UNDEFEATED
FATE OF THE WOLF GUARD

AIDY AWARD

Copyright © 2022 by Aidy Award

All rights reserved.

No part of this book may be reproduced in any form or by any electronic or mechanical means, including information storage and retrieval systems, without written permission from the author, except for the use of brief quotations in a book review.

❦ Created with Vellum

For all the women who give everything of themselves and ask nothing in return.
Quit it.
Don't sacrifice everything because you fear losing love if you don't.
Ask.
Those that love you will be happy to return that love to you, and those that don't... fuck 'em.

Her enemy is loneliness or isolation.

— GAIL CARRIGER

TARYN

I am not going down without a fight.

I have been a sister, a daughter, a priestess, a tsarina, a queen, and now I am a fucking goddess and a true mate to four sexy, amazing, delicious guards. No one, not even the god of chaos is going to take that away from me.

This giant demon owl form Nergal has taken may have me in its talons flying around like an unhinged chicken who caught the magic worm, aka me, but I refuse to freak out.

Why? Because my mates are here, all four of them, back together again, and that above all else gives me strength. I've learned that when I use my magic in a knee jerk reaction kind of way, I don't always like the consequences.

I'm going to breathe through the pain and figure out how to escape without killing anyone this time. Although, it would sure as shit help if I had a clue how to control my powers, or even what they all were. Somehow I don't think the ability to heal or turn into a werewolf is going to help me escape Nergal's powerful talons.

I let out a growl anyway and kick and jerk around, half hoping he'll drop me. I bring up one of my blue balls of magic, but don't know where to aim it. I don't really want to go crashing to the ground, but maybe I can get that new black dragon dude we've pulled onto Team Taryn to catch me. He looks pretty damn grumpy for someone who's just escaped Hell, so maybe not. "Let me go, you foul fowl, or I'll pluck your feathers out one by one."

Nergal squawks or screeches or whatever it is he does, and is unperturbed by my threats. Fine. I toss my magic up into the air, directly in his path, hoping it defeathers him as is my intention. Instead of doing a thing to hurt him, hundreds of moon flowers sprout along the branches of the trees.

Great. That's useful.

Dammit. I just spent an eternity in a dungeon forced to use my own wit and magic. Come on, powerful inner strength, let's get this show on the road. What else can I try? Opening a portal comes to mind, but those have all just led to Hell and what got me into this crapload of trouble in the first place. We just finished eviscerating all his demon wyrm buddies, I don't want to let more out into the world.

I also have the uncanny ability to make people shift

into their human forms, but they're always naked, and I have no desire to be anywhere Nergal's peen. Blech. Which means, I'm loath to use my other magic powers. The kind that pours out of my eyes, ears, fingers, toes, nose... and vagina.

See? Yeah. No. My vagina and Nergal do not go together. Ever.

Nergal may have me in his grasp but I'll figure out how to get away, in another couple of seconds. I take another deep breath and remember where my abilities come from. Even the thought of August, Vas, and Grigori marking me and making me theirs gets me all tingly with magic and more than a little lust.

Even though I haven't yet mated with Joachim, I know he's mine too. He cares deeply for me, but has forbidden himself from fulfilling the bond between us. After this, I'm not going to let him keep anything between us. I am not fricking dying again to be reincarnated without my mates. Nope. Nuh-uh. Nyet.

The power rises inside of me like moonlight shining through the clouds. What I see in the darkness around us gives me a lump of dread in my throat. A gray shimmer of magic emanates all around me and Nergal. It is like a fine layer of dust and I can feel it gripping both of us.

And it's coming from Rasputin.

Yeah. That Rasputin. The one who controlled the last Tzar of Russia because he was in love with the Tsarina. My memories of him are strange and spotty, but there's one thing I know for sure. He's a dickmunch if I ever knew one. Worse than Peter, even. Makes me wonder if dumb old Petey was in league with the Volkovs. He probably was.

How and why this band of wolves came into power and decided they got to rule my people is what I don't understand. I remember almost everything about who I am and my hundreds of past lives now, but not how and where the Volkovs came from.

Rasputin is not a god. He is one of my people. I gave him the gift of shifting into a wolf, as I did all who descended from those who worshiped me in the beginning times. That piece of my own soul, my magic, doesn't give him or his buddies this kind of power.

"Bring her to me, Nergal so we can be done with this." Rasputin raises his arms, and if I squint just right, I think I can see a tether of magic pulling on Nergal. That's some weird bullshit right there.

Grigori gives me a mental push. *Princess, shift, use the abilities you've mastered to free yourself.*

My wolves are surrounding Rasputin, but they aren't attacking. All eyes are on me. Is this my everyday life here on this island hellhole? Fight, recover, only to fight again? I don't accept that. My one goal since the day I popped out on the beach with no memory of who or what I am, was to escape this prison. I am taking each and every man, woman, wolf... and lion, and whatever Maggie is, with me too.

The Volkovs, our jailers, don't get to decide who is

good and who isn't. Rasputin wouldn't know a moral compass if it bit him on the schlong.

Instead of using my powers, since I don't feel fully in control of them, I'm going to try an age-old tactic. "Hey Nergally Wergally. I always knew Ereshkigal had you under her thumb, but now you're letting the mealy-mouthed Rasputin hold your leash too?"

Negral makes a weird growly screechy sound that sounds more like a dying pigeon and Rasputin throws death glares at me.

Men like these two, who have to puff themselves up and try to control others, are the ones with the most sensitive egos. My time as Russian royalty taught me that. I ruled all of Russia as Katherine the Great, started a revolution as Princess Sophia Alekseyevna, and burned down the world around the men who thought they could control me as Olga of Kiev. I can certainly take down one minor god and a defunct monk.

Nergal screeches like the underworld bird-thing that he is and it definitely sounds like an avian version of 'fuck you'. That's exactly what I want to hear. But strange that he didn't try to mind-speak. I'm pretty sure gods and goddesses can do that whenever we want.

"Yeah, that's right, ya big schmoe. He's got you by the short and, uh, featheries, doesn't he? You and I could take him on, don't let him control you." The more I talk, the better I can see that Nergal isn't himself. Rasputin's control over him is a dangerous element in this battle for all of us. When he breaks free of the leash holding him, someone is going to die.

That needs to be Rasputin, not me or my family and friends.

Nergal takes my bait and swoops down, dive bombing the ground. I scream out of pure instinct and surprisingly that's what gets him to drop me. I would have screamed my head off from the get-go if I'd known he was startled by that.

I'm just about to release a stream of magic to cushion my fall when another set of talons snags me out of mid-air. What the shit?

Jett is on our side, Boginya. Don't fight him. August's calm but commanding voice takes me from a level eleventy-hundred on the what-the-hell scale to the usual. Except he's flying me away from the fight. He's got me cupped in his claw so I could jump out if I wanted to, but if August says he's working with us, I'll believe him.

I grab a hold of his leg and point toward the battle. "Wait, where are you going? We can't leave my wolves."

It's not like they can't defend themselves, but I don't want even another minute of separation from them. I just got August and Vas back. We didn't even have time to say hello, I love you, I missed you, I'm so glad you're not dead and can't wait to get back in your pants.

The dragon swoops in a wide arc, turning us back around, but keeping us at a distance. At least I can see what's going on. Nergal is literally pecking at Rasputin as if he is no more than the giant bird he appears to be.

Whatever magical tether Rasputin has on him, has a hold of his true powers. The guy is a god of the underworld for goodness sake.

Rasputin is asking for a smiting. Ooh. That sounds fun. I should try doing that. I rub my hands together to juice my powers up and shoot a stream of light right at Rasputin. I was hoping more for a bolt of lightning, but whatever. Maybe next time.

The beam of light shoots toward him, but right before it gets there, it splits in four and gives each of my wolves a shot of my magic. Shit. The last time I did something like that, they all turned human, and drooly, half-conscious ones at that.

This time, only Father Joachim shifts back into his human form. He looks up at me from the ground, once again butt naked except for his prayer beads, with a quizzical look on his face. If I wasn't being flown through the air by a fricking dragon, I'd shrug, because damned if I know why that happened. "Sorry, my bad, Father."

I shoot another quick burst of magic at him and he shifts back once again. At least I know how to do one thing right. Right-ish.

My magical fuck-up has given Rasputin time to get his poop in a group. He shoves Nergal away and drops his own robes. Blurgh. I've never seen anyone, much less a wolf-shifter, so wrinkly and bone thin. But his wolf form pops out as his skin and bones break and reform just like anyone else, and his wolf is big and intimidating. Uh-oh.

"Dragon dude, put me down, I need to help them."

Dragon dude does not put me down. He flies up a little higher. Dammit. From this angle I can see everything happening in one glance.

Rasputin lowers his head in a stance that looks like he's ready to attack, but is slowly backing away. Ooh, without Nergal as his weapon, he's frightened of my wolf guard. Good to know. Vas lunges, but too late. Nergal scoops up Rasputin just like he did me, and tosses him right into the trees. Well, well, well. Isn't that interesting?

Vas and August stalk in the direction Rasputin careened, but Grigori stops them. He shifts and the others follow suit. If they're having a confab, I want in on it. I tug on the big dragon leg as if I can steer him back to the battle ground. "Take me back down now, please. I'll give you a dragon treat if you will."

The dragon makes a sound that I'm pretty sure is a snort-laugh. Rude. August waves up to us, and sure, fine, that's when the dragon dude decides to take me back down. He's got some kind of loyalty to August, so I guess I'll forgive him.

When we land, I run straight into August's arms and pull Vas into our group hug. If they're happy to stand around in their more vulnerable, and not to mention naked, human forms, they must not be worried about Rasputin anymore. I'm happy to take advantage of the moment.

"I'm so, so, so, so sorry I accidentally sent you both to Hell. I swear I was trying to help. I thought I'd killed you." The tears are bubbling up and dribbling over my eyelashes totally uncontrolled. August responds by peppering kisses and licks across the mark he gave me, sending shivers up and down my spine.

Vas tucks himself against me and wraps one arm around my waist so tight, I think he'll never let me go. Which is fine by me. He shoves the other hand into my hair and cups the back of my head, tilting my face up to him. His eyes are burning with the wolf inside of him. I see no hurt there, only lust and relief. He brushes his lips softly across mine, but leaves me with a nip to my bottom lip that promises more.

Grigori clears his throat. "We can all have a naked reunion later. Let's get Taryn back to the *derevenya* while Nergal and Rasputin are having their spat and figure out what the fuck we do next."

I know what we need to do. "We need to get everyone off this island, and for that we need me to be at full power."

August smiles down at me. "You remember now who and what you are, don't you?"

"There's a few holes still in my Swiss cheese of a brain, but I think if you all fill in some of the missing details, I can use my powers to finally break the spell or curse or whatever is holding us all here. Isn't that right, Father Joachim?" I spring that last bit on him. He's still keeping both his true self and secrets from me. I haven't wanted to force his hand up until now.

That's a little bit of a lie. I've pushed him into doing what he claimed he wasn't ready for multiple times. That needs to end now. He's mine, and I am his, and there's a freedom in that which we've all been waiting for. All eyes turn to him.

He fingers the prayer beads and nods his head. "Yes, *Boginya*. It's time I repented for my sins against you. Against you all."

JOACHIM

On the retreat to the *derevnya*, I let Grigori, August, and Vasily keep watch over Taryn and her dragon ride. I need a few moments to compose myself. Few times in my life have I known real fear. That base emotion was trained out of me once I submitted myself to be a priest to the Goddess of the Moon.

I learned to fight for her, pray to her, live and die for her. None of it would I give up for even a moment. It's everything that came after that I regret.

My actions, my hubris, is what fucked us all. And she's about to find out.

I have known since the very first death and rebirth that the only way to break this curse is for all five of us to be together again. For centuries, I've wondered how the Volkovs have ensured that no more than three of us were with her in any given life. Now I see I wasn't the only one who made a deal with the devil.

Seeing Rasputin use her power to tether the consort of the underworld has shaken me and my faith to the very core.

I can no longer keep my transgressions against her and my fellow Guards a secret. But by admitting everything to her now, I could also be putting her ascendance into jeopardy. Why would she ever want to take me as her mate, when I'm the cause of all of our problems for the past five-thousand years?

I am so fucked.

I have to tell her, tell the rest of them, but it's a secret I've kept for so long, that it's buried deep in my soul. The truth will either set us free or destroy us. Damned if I do, damned if I don't.

If she forgives me it will be a miracle. If August, Vasily, and Grigori do, well, that's more than I can ever hope for. I haven't forgiven myself. Why would they?

If they would have all followed my plan to mate with her at once, when August claimed her, maybe it wouldn't have come to this. Once again, I thought I knew best, and once again the universe showed me just how wrong I was. One would think I'd learn my damned lesson and stop making the same mistakes.

Only in her light, can I be healed.

Grigori gives me a mental poke, and I realize the dragon flies faster than I expect and I've fallen too far behind. None of us know how long Nergal and Rasputin will take to battle over who controls whom. The faster I act, the better.

My wolf pushes at me in ways I haven't allowed it to in centuries. I used to be able to rely on the rituals of the one-God faith I adopted to control myself and my urges. But not anymore. Prayer only goes so far. Especially when it's to the wrong God. She is the only one I've ever truly worshiped.

Mark.

Claim.

Mate.

The ever present lust I feel for her rises up, spurring me to hurry to her side. I likely have precious little time left with her before she casts me out, so I quicken my pace to be there when the black dragon lands in the center of the *derevnya*.

Will, in his great lion form, with Maggie by his side as always, waits for us. He paces like the predator that he is and it's not hard to sense his unease at a beast from Hell entering his domain. Many of the other wolves shift into their animal forms, ready to defend and attack if need be, but they hold off because of Taryn.

I shift and hold up my hands to calm those waiting. "Please, be calm. The dragon is our ally, and we'll need all we can get this day."

My own life may be on the verge of utter destruction, but I will still do all that I can to minister to the forgotten and downtrodden of this island. Too many have been cast in here spuriously by the Volkovs and Taryn's presence has given them the only hope they've known.

The dragon lands and carefully opens its talons,

allowing Taryn to crawl out. She smiles and waves to Maggie, and that in and of itself, calms everyone around us much more than my placating words. A moment later, August, Vas, and Grigori come up on either side of her and they shift too.

"Can someone get these hunka-hunks some robes? We've got a lot to talk about and nobody needs to be distracted by their, uh... butts."

August grins at her in a way that's so easy I want to groan for wanting the same with her. *Sweet princess, I would happily do each and every one of those things to you right here and now if we weren't fresh out of Hell with a war on our hands.*

Taryn's mental images of all five of us naked and worshiping her body are projected right into our heads. She never was any good at hiding her feelings, or her wanton lusts. She hides a blush by handing over robes that some of her newfound friends provide.

I've squandered too many lives denying myself the pleasure of making her blush and an ache pounds deep in my belly. The sooner I tell her everything, the less I have to live with these pangs of guilt manifesting as actual pain. Either she will forgive me or she won't. Either I'll continue to be her Wolf Guard, or she'll cast me out. Either I will be allowed to be her mate once again, or... more than likely not.

There can be no in between. She loves me despite my transgressions, or we all suffer for my hubris.

Grigori gives me a sideways glance and even without

saying anything, he knows something is amiss. "We need to gather as many fighters together as we can. Rasputin and Nergal are here and they're after Taryn."

A gasp goes through the gathering. Rasputin is the one who sentenced most of them to this prison and many fear him and his powers. Powers he never should have had in the first place.

"Who is Nergal?" A younger wolftress steps forward and asks what many are wondering. The stories of our Gods and Goddesses are centuries old, and mostly forgotten, in the absence of no one to worship them like in the ancient days.

I doubt anyone but the five of us, and perhaps Will and Maggie, know much about any of the ancient gods and goddesses. They barely know the tales of the Goddess of the Moon and it's become only folklore. They are in for an awakening. Assuming we all survive the day.

Even I am loath to speak about Nergal in an open forum this way. Taryn is the one who finally says something. "He's an asshat is who he is. If you see a big, ugly owl flying around here, I guess, hide. He's bad news."

"But is he a Volkov, or one of their minions, or something else?"

It's useless to keep them in the dark, seeing as they will be fighting him soon. I step forward, next to Taryn, wanting to be near her. "Nergal is the God of Chaos, and the consort to Ereshkigal, Goddess of the Underworld."

"That sounds bad. Why is he here? Can he hurt us, kill us? Is he working for the Volkovs?" The crowd gathers closer and peppers Taryn and I with questions. They're frightened and she is the closest thing they have to a safe place.

Grigori growls, letting his wolf rise up and it doesn't take long for everyone to back off. They don't yet trust him. Only Taryn's presence makes it okay. They trust her implicitly without even knowing why.

Taryn puts her hand on his shoulder and soothes his savage beast for all to see. His quick glance her way shines with the deep abiding love he has for her. "It's okay, my prince. They're just scared."

"They have nothing to be scared of. We have kept you and your people safe from the machinations of the gods for centuries. We will not fail them now." He scoffs as if they should all know who and what we are. They don't even yet know she is their Queen, their Goddess.

"Okay, so let's make sure they feel protected. Do your thing. Alpha it up." She looks out over her people and gives them a smile. "I know this is asking a lot, but I need you to do exactly as my Guards ask of you. We need some time to come up with a plan to free us all from this dumb island. We can't do that if we're worried you aren't safe."

Her skin sparkles and shimmers with the blue light of her power as she speaks. She was always at her most powerful when she was taking care of her people.

"You've got this, my queen." Grigori takes a step back, but Taryn grabs his hand.

"I know I do, but if I've learned anything recently, it's that I don't want to do anything alone, ever again. Help me. Each of you, help me make them safe from Nergal and Rasputin."

I doubt she even realizes, but moon flowers are sprouting up out of the ground around her and the clouds above us are parting, exposing the blue sky for the first time. In an instant, the cold frost of Siberian spring melts, and warmth like we haven't known on the island invades us all.

It doesn't take long for people to realize the pure awesomeness of who she is. In a fast moving wave, starting with those directly in front of us, her people drop to their knees, and bow their heads before her.

"Wait, no. That's not what I want. Please don't bow to me. Get up, and let's work together." Taryn squats down and lifts her friend Alida by the arm, then Bridget, and Killisi. "You're my friends, not... worshippers. You've saved me so many times already. I need you, all of you, if we're going to finally get off this island."

Alida was the first to move and accept Taryn's proffered request. It didn't take the other girls long to follow suit. Once they did, the rest of the crowd joined, although most were still in awe. I understood. The first time I got a glimpse of her power, I'd prostrated myself before her too.

It was time I did so again. "Ladies, as her trusted friends, can you organize the people and packs? Most need to go into hiding, with a few to keep watch."

"We'll take care of everything." Alida gave a dip of her chin to me, and a shy smile to Taryn. Before she turned away, she asked, "Do you truly believe you can end our imprisonment?"

Taryn took a deep breath and the light around her brightened even more. "I'm going to do everything in my power."

Maggie waved the wolftresses off and wrapped arms with Taryn. "It's so good to see the real you, love. Now come inside, we'll make a cuppa, and you all can get to work on your plans."

Taryn tipped her head to the side and looked Maggie deep in the eyes, then her eyebrows went up and she let out a small laugh. "It's good to see the real you, too."

The two went into Maggie's cabin and the rest of us looked back and forth among each other. Will broke the silence. "Yes, your Goddess knows what my Maggie is. None of the rest of you lot need to, so shut your open traps before the flies get in. We've got battle plans to make. This should be fun."

We filed in and while it was cramped, there was room for me to stand before what would be my tribunal. I didn't know how to begin.

Grigori helped me along the way by asking the question everyone wanted to know. "How has Nergal found her now, after all these years? He stopped hunting for her upon her first rebirth."

August nodded. "I thought since she didn't go to the underworld she was somehow safe. Is it because Vas and I were in Hell? Did he find her through us?"

A flash of guilt passed through Vas's eyes, and above

all, I couldn't take that. Vasily had dealt with his own worries that he'd let her down for the last hundred years, he didn't need this on his conscience. Not when I could save him the heartache.

It was time. I wasn't strong enough, but I had to be.

"I alone know the answer to that question." As I expected, all eyes turned to me. The three men that meant the world to me, the ones I fought and loved beside, waiting on my explanation. The guilt bubbled up inside of me and I tasted the bitterness of my betrayal in the back of my throat.

Grigori motioned for me to continue.

I couldn't.

I must.

"August is correct that when Taryn died in that first life, and was reincarnated, that she and her powers were then hidden from Nergal."

"That's what we all wanted. To keep her safe." Vas said.

Taryn scrunched up her eyes and it didn't take her long to fill in the memory. "He was trying to capture me, wasn't he?"

"He would have done the unspeakable to you if he'd succeeded. Our powers were nothing compared to his, and we were desperate to keep you safe."

"I was weak, from giving up a part of myself to my people so they had the ability to defend themselves. His demons were the ones who persecuted us, killing everyone. I knew he was an asshat."

Grigori's lips thinned as he looked at me. "We've always guessed, but how do you know? And if her powers have been hidden all this time, how has he found her now?"

"Because I'm the one who gave her powers away, and took her life."

TARYN

Father Joachim, my priest, since the beginning of time, my most trusted advisor, the man that I want as my mate, and my guard, gave away my powers?

And killed me?

I can't...

No, no, no, no. This can't be true, and yet, somewhere in the darkest depths of my incomplete memories, I remember.

I was in my temple, bathing in the moonlight, trying to rebuild my energy and my power knowing Nergal was coming for me. Joachim came to me, he held me, kissed me, brought me pleasure as we relished each other's bodies...

And then there is nothing.

Wait. Not nothing. A searing pain, and then nothing.

"You..." My voice comes out barely loud enough to hear. "What did you do?"

Grigori, Vas, and August are all standing there staring at Joachim like he's a ghost, or a demon himself. Grigori is the first to recover and he jumps forward and pins Joachim against the nearest wall. He growls and his wolf rises up, his claws extend and his fangs drop as he partially shifts. "Yes, Joachim, what did you do?"

Joachim gives me a look that makes me ache inside with emotions that are both mine and not my own. I should interfere, stop Grigori from hurting him. I just... don't. It's not that I want to see him in pain, but my arms and legs have gone numb. But this pain projecting from him, it's made my mouth, vocal chords, and lungs stop functioning. I'm broken.

Everyone else is frozen, or not willing to get between the two of them.

Father Joachim doesn't fight against Grigori's death grip on him either, and I think that more than anything is what stops the Dark Prince from tearing his head off.

Vas gets himself back together after this bomb and is the only one to act in the way that I should. He puts a hand on Grigori's wrist, the one around Father Joachim's throat. "We will hear what he has to say. There is more to his story than that simple confession."

Grigori growls and his words are barely intelligible. "How do you know? Were you in on this conspiracy? Am I the only one who doesn't know what the fuck is going on here?"

I can literally feel Grigori's anger, like little spears poking me from the inside out. Yet I still can't move. I flash August a look trying to ask him to help with my eyes alone. Not only does my voice not work, even my mental voice that allows me to share my thoughts and feelings with my mates is broken too.

August apparently doesn't need me to say anything, and I am ridiculously grateful that he understood. With nothing more than a nod, he steps up to the other side and puts his hand across Vas's and folds over Grigori's grip. Slowly, he pulls the fingers off, and Grigori lets him, but with a snarl. "Let him speak, Grigori. Taryn wishes it."

Grigori glares at me, but takes a step back. Father Joachim doesn't even move a centimeter from the wall, even though he's free. His back is still ramrod straight and his eyes are a storm. The wolf is right there, but he's not allowing it out.

"No one else was involved in my mistake that has betrayed you all. It is mine alone to bear."

Grigori growls and turns away. Father Joachim takes two harsh breaths. This discordance is literally paining him and that in turn hurts me. I don't like the idea that we're not all on the same side. I want to fix it, and I can't. I can't.

Joachim reaches out for me, and I shrink away. "Please, *boginya,* understand I didn't do any of this to harm you. Everything I did was to keep you safe from Nergal. You were weakened and we were not yet strong enough to protect you."

August asked the question that I couldn't seem to get out of my throat, even though I was desperate to know. "What exactly is it that you did?"

I thought I knew everything about each of my guards now that I had most of my memories back. But now I realize that there are some distinct blank spaces when it comes to the Father. I thought that was only because we hadn't yet claimed each other and become true mates.

In fact, we hadn't bonded that way in several lifetimes. Is this secret he's been holding onto a blade between us? It hurts like a dagger to my heart, and it isn't something I can forgive easily.

Father Joachim avoids looking at me, bowing his head. He clicks the prayer beads at his waist and they take on an eerie glow, a blue light similar to my own magic. His voice is almost a whisper, but I can hear him as if his mouth is right next to my ear. "I made a deal with Rasputin."

Grigori jumps and slams Joachim against the wall again. August and Vas grab him by the shoulders to restrain him, and all of their wolves are so near the surface it would be only a moment before they all shift and tear each other apart. For me.

But none of this feels as though I am their queen and they are my guards, consorts, lovers. This is hell. Worse.

I raise my hand and they are all still. I still can't seem to find my voice again, and I don't think I will. Not until Father Joachim tells me everything. Then I can breathe again.

He opens his mouth and then closes it. His memories are thousands of years old and he's lived almost as many lives as I have in all that time. Somehow though, I don't think these events have faded from his mind. He takes a shallow breath and then brings his eyes up to mine.

"I used our access to you, and the way you opened yourself to give us the gift of your magic, to siphon off that which attracted Nergal to you. But it wasn't enough. Even with all but the tiniest drops of magic, you still glowed like the moon in the night sky. You were a beacon for Nergal's dark and chaotic soul."

He held his prayer beads aloft. "So, I went to the last place I thought Hell would go to look for you."

How clever my priest is.

Grigori snarled. "You fucker, you took her power to the priests of Ereshkigal herself?"

Grigori made the same intuitive leap as me. Nergal may be a god, but he is forever beholden to his queen, the Goddess of the Underworld. Joachim hid my power in plain sight.

"Nergal would never suspect the acolytes of Ereshkigal as the hiding place of the object of his desire. Even if he did, he wouldn't dare torment them." For the first time since the beginning of his sordid tale, Joachim's wolf shines in his eyes. His inner strength doesn't waver, even under the onslaught of his guilt at having caused us all so much pain. "And I was right. She's been hidden from him for five thousand years. Until now."

"I remember." Funny how something that happened

five thousand years ago could be both fuzzy in my mind and also as clear as if it happened yesterday. "You came to me in the temple at Ur. I was tired and weak, and you laid with me, tried to give me strength through your love. But there's nothing after that."

It was as if I fell asleep, but when I reawakened, everything was different. I was an infant, newly born and the world was bright and confusing. My life as I knew over, and a mortal life started anew.

Grigori fills in the next part. "We all died that night, though none of us should have. You bound us to your immortality so that we could be by your side as eternal companions, lovers, and protectors of you and your light."

Vas shakes his head and takes a step back. The hurt wolf I met on the shore on my first night flashes through his eyes and I think if I weren't standing here folded in on myself and needing him by my side, he might retreat to his beast once again. "We've all wondered life after life what curse befell us, and all along it was you, Joachim?"

Joachim ignores everyone else and stares only at me. "Your death sealed the spell. Rasputin swore that when we all reawakened, you would be safe from Nergal. He may have become a greedy despot who used your power for his own gain, but in that he did not lie."

The first time I saw any of my guards again, Grigori and Joachim only, I'd been a poor, but happy little peasant girl, no cares, no enemies, no demons of the underworld chasing me, trying to devour me and my powers.

No magic, no people worshiping me, no one to be a goddess for.

"You murdered her. You took her magic, you took her from us and her people." Grigori's anger rises up again, and this time, I find the strength inside of me to quell the rage.

I open that part of me that's been asleep for far too long. I connect to August, Vasily, and Grigori, feeling the love and connection between us. They are all the keepers of my magic, of my power, not Rasputin. Moonlight fills the room and settles first onto Grigori's shoulders, soaking in until his muscles unbunch and his mind calms.

He bows his head, shakes it, his disappointment, hurt, and sadness palpable. He comes to my side, takes my hand and kisses it, finally understanding that at least in this fight, I don't need his protection, only his support.

Vas comes to my side, then August joins, flanking my back. They are my strength, because of their love for me, and mine for them. We are a team, more even, because when we are all as one, we are an unbreakable force.

We cannot all be together as we are meant to be without Joachim, and right now, there is too much hurt flowing between us all for that to happen.

However, Joachim is wrong in one aspect of his story. Rasputin had lied to him.

His death spell may have hidden me from Nergal, but he hadn't taken my power. He simply used what I'd already gifted him as one of my people, along with the gifts he must have received from Ereshkigal when he became one of her priests.

I understand how that would appear to be an overabundance of my magic. He'd used it to his advantage, not allowing all four of my guards to be reincarnated into any of my own lives, thus keeping a part of my memories eternally bound.

While Joachim didn't believe in the strength of the five of us united, I did.

I too am hurt and angry at the way Joachim decided to act without talking to the rest of us, that he thought he knew what was best for us all. To me, that was his greater sin, the rest could be forgiven. He'd done it all to protect me and keep me safe.

But he hadn't thought I, his Goddess, his Queen, was strong enough to do that for myself. Nor that my chosen ones, the guardians of me, my heart, my power, my soul, were smart enough, strong enough to keep me safe.

Joachim looks between the four of us and drops to his knees in front of me. "Please, *boginya*, forgive me. I have committed too many sins to expect your favor ever again, but I can't help but ask for it."

I breathe in, I breathe out. The power inside of me swells and my body reacts to his nearness. He is mine, and he always will be, but… I don't know how to be with him. He's sorry he hurt me, hurt us, and yet he doesn't entirely believe what he did was wrong.

I reach down and cup his chin, tilting his head up. He

defers his eyes down so low, it's as if they are closed. "Look at me, Guard of the Divided moon."

His gaze snaps up to mine.

"I can forgive everything you did in trying to protect me." I end my first sentence on a cool note. They are all waiting for some kind of verdict from me.

His face falls because he sees that my forgiveness isn't complete, as much as he's hoped it would be. I am not his false god who forgives those who confess their sins.

"Because you did all of that out of love for me. What hurts me is that you alone decided how to best keep me safe. Without one another we are nothing. How can I trust you with my heart, my body, and the safe-keeping of the Divided moon if you don't trust in me?"

"My goddess, I swear on my very soul, that I will not—"

"Words are not enough, Joachim." I'm not having it. I've spent plenty of time among men with excuses of why they thought they knew better. That more than anything else is what disappoints me. That's not who I thought he was. "You've spent five thousand years demonstrating to all of us that you didn't believe we were worthy of your trust. You could have told me and Grigori what happened in the very first life and hundreds of times since, yet, only now when we would have found out anyway, did you finally admit what you've done."

He jerks his chin, trying to break eye contact with me, but I don't allow it. He blinks, but if he is trying to hold back his emotions, it doesn't work. They pool and then drip from the side of his eyes.

"I'm sorry, my goddess. So sorry. I have failed you more than I ever realized. I'm so sorry."

My spine, my heart, my very soul, tingles with pins and needles. I absolutely hate this discord between us all. I want nothing more than to wrap him in my arms and tell him everything will be fine. But right now, I'm not sure anything will ever be okay between us again. I can't fix this with simple love and forgiveness. "I know."

The whooshing of great bird wings sounds outside, and the respite we had ends with a new battle to be fought.

I squeeze my hands into fists. "This isn't over, but we must fight off the forces of Hell and greed once again. I don't want anyone else hurt by our fight, so it's time we get everyone off this damn island. Once my people are safe from Nergal and Rasputin, then we will figure out our fates."

GRIGORI

A shadow passes over the windows and we hear Nergal's screech. The bastard has horrible timing and if I could I'd rip his feathers out one by one and roast him on a spit over an open fire. But Gods are hard to kill.

I touch Taryn's mind with my own, and do what I can in that brief moment to make sure she knows she is still loved. She's closed herself off and I can only sense her hurt and her need to escape. One I can't do anything about, but I will make sure she can get off this island. I'll kill Rasputin and send Nergal back to Hell if I have to take him there myself.

Except my sweet princess has taught me that I'm not alone in my duty. We have friends among the people here who are on our side. Without Joachim, we're going to need all the help we can get.

"Will, you and Mags defend the barn, we may need it for triage." Will nods, allowing me to take the lead, even though this *derevnya* is his domain and has been for a very long time. Maggie takes his hand and I hate that such a solid, loving couple has to see the lowest point in our relationship. We'll never have what they do. Not now.

"August, Vas, get out there and don't let those pack alphas fuck up the plan. The last thing we need is more chaos." I really didn't even need to tell the two of them what to do. They react instantly, both giving Taryn a brief kiss before shifting and bounding out the door. I need that extra minute to think. Never before have I worried that I couldn't completely trust one of our own.

Joachim has been a complete fuckwad for the last five thousand years and I can't believe I didn't know or even have a clue. Taryn's hurt seeps through our connection and digs deep into the armor I have around my own anger. I don't want her feeling any of that. She doesn't need to contend with my emotions too.

I've never been one to coddle her, but it is my duty to keep her out of danger, and it'snot fucking safe right now.

Without him, she won't be able to fully regain her powers and ascend to her rightful place as Queen and Goddess. If that wasn't the case, I'd already have his throat torn out and be feasting on his betraying heart. Out of anyone in this forsaken existence, he's the last person I would have expected this from.

All those years I trusted him with the darkest parts of

my soul and he couldn't do the same.

When this is over, regardless of the outcome, I will rip his fucking head off and feed it to the wyrms. Unfortunately for us all, we still need him. Especially right now when Nergal is once again attacking.

No way I'm sending Joachim into battle with the Volkov he'd made a goddess-damned deal with. He turns toward the door as if he's leaving. My wolf rises up, wanting to shift and make him supplicate himself to me, make him show me his throat. I don't suppress the warning growl that rumbles up from my chest.

Joachim freezes, bows his head, and slowly turns back. "I will defend and protect her, Grigori, whether you want me to or not. I will not allow more harm to come to her on my watch."

We both know that I can use my alpha voice and demand his obedience. That won't fix a damn thing. He isn't worthy of being in my presence, much less my pack. I won't deign to use the power of the alpha within me on him.

I'd rather let my wolf eat his fucking face. It's clawing to get out, and the only reason I can keep in the rage my beast wants to unleash is the utter despair in Taryn's eyes. I can taste her bitter sorrow in the back of my throat. "It isn't your watch any longer. Stand down."

Instead of doing as he should, Joachim stands up straighter, his own wolf glowing in his eyes. "I will not let Rasputin or Nergal touch her, not now, not ever again."

"You should have thought of that when you were

making your deal with devils." I expect my words to hurt him, but he doesn't even flinch. He's gone numb to my anger and that pisses me off even more. "I'd kill you here and now if I didn't know the consequences. Defend your own life so that she may decide your fate. I am done with you."

I've bared everything to Joachim time and time again, as a leader in need of counsel, and as a man who needed a friend. Turns out I got nothing in return but platitudes.

I don't wait for his response or even Taryn's. I've got shit to take care of. We need more time to figure out how to enact Taryn's wishes to save the souls on this island and I need her safe.

Nergal and Rasputin are incoming and we don't have the time we need. Joachim picked a fine time to destroy our world. I didn't think it could get any worse than it's been for the past hundred or so years without her in it. But he's done it, he's eviscerated the last remaining bit of faith I have.

How the fuck will she accept him as her fourth mate and guardian? I don't want him anywhere near her... or me. Yet without him, she can't realize her full self and ascend to her goddess state and powers. The only way off this island is a portal, and without her full powers, that's not happening. Unless we'd all rather live out the end of our lives in Hell. Fuck.

Fuck.

Fucking.

Fucker.

I slam the door shut and breathe in the cool spring air. Taryn's magic is at work all around me and I breathe it in, needing her strength more than ever. I've walked into a battle in progress, but the fight and adrenaline is muted. I must shake this utter betrayal off or I'll make a stupid mistake. We've got a war to win against Hell.

Nergal swoops high in the sky above us, in some kind of waiting game. Rasputin must have regained his control. But where is he? Gathering more allies from Hell or perhaps bringing in more slaves made loyal to the Volkovs?

Taryn yanks the door open behind me, and when I spin to shove her back inside, the wind is blowing through her hair, the light is shining down on her, or maybe the light is coming from her. I can't tell because even without her full powers, she is the embodiment of the Goddess of the Moon, and I'm awed by her.

"I can't afford to lose anyone else. That includes you." She pokes me in the chest. "Don't go off doing anything dumb, my Dark Prince."

"I'm not the one who did something stupid, my queen." I try to look behind her, to glare at Joachim, but she moves to block the doorway.

"That's debatable. I think I could make an argument for quite a few things you've done that weren't so smart." She folds her arms and a warm wind whips around me. Stars above, I fucking love her so damned much.

She's not wrong. I spent the last hundred years tearing the world around me down because I couldn't have her.

That's the reminder I need that through her, all things are possible. Even when I don't see how we can possibly go on to defeat our enemies, both the ones we face on the field of battle and the ones within ourselves.

I grab her and pull her into my arms, needing her more than anything else. She lets out a startled gasp and I swallow the sound as I take her mouth, crushing our lips together. She doesn't melt in my arms, no, not my queen. Taryn kisses me back with all the fervor of our first kiss, but with so much more love behind it.

I want to live in this moment forever, forget about everyone else, and revel in her, her body, her love. But the battle is oncoming, and we break our kiss short. She touches my cheek and looks so deep into my eyes, I'm sure she's looking directly into my dark soul. "This is what I need, more than protection. I don't know how to do what I must without all of you by my side and in my heart."

In that plea, and that's what it is, a request from her heart to mine, there is the vision of the future she needs. I must be strong enough to help her grasp it. "It is exactly what we all need. Even fucking Joachim."

I don't know that I can ever forgive him. But maybe she can.

Her eyes flick back and forth over mine and I see the gears in her mind working. "I... I don't know how to be with him."

"You'll figure it out." I leave part of what she needs to hear unsaid. I can't simply tell her she still has to mate with him, claim him and be claimed by him, so that she can ascend.

Shouts come from the far end of the *derevnya* and we both look, even though I know full well the battle is beginning without me. I release her, though she doesn't entirely let me go.

"I will save them, Grigori. But I'm going to need your help, and August's, and Vas's, because I know what I have to do and I don't know if I can."

I didn't know either. I could never again trust Joachim with anything, how could she trust him with a claim and her body? I couldn't placate her this time, although my sentiment that she could figure it out for herself was sincere. She didn't and shouldn't have to. That is why she had us in the first place. We are a team, a unit, four hearts beating as one. Five was better.

"You don't have to save everyone right this moment. Let's get rid of the imminent threat and then we can all drag Joachim over the coals and we'll decide what you want to do with him after that."

She gave a small grimace and a shake of her head. There was so much more to this than my oversimplified solution, and we both knew it. Emotions and empathy aren't my strong suit and I was shit at doing this kind of caring for her.

Joachim was the one we all turned to for this.

I am strategy, action, and utter belief in my goddess. "Come, let's throw some chaos back at Nergal and see how he likes it."

We leave Joachim behind in the cabin and dash over to where August and Vas are forming our first line of defense. They've got the dragon warrior who'd joined forces with them in Hell and he's shifted to his human form. I'm wary of any beast of Hell, but they've got a bond with him and he did help keep Taryn out of harm's way. He may be useful to us in this ongoing fight.

Taryn looks around at the wolves gathered to protect her and the *derevnya*. "I don't like this. I don't want anyone hurt. I'm supposed to be protecting them, not the other way around."

"They won't have to fight. You're going to open a bunch of portals to Hell, let's see if we can throw Nergal off guard and back to Hell." Then we'll deal with Rasputin wolf to wolf.

"No, but the demon wyrms will come again." Taryn looks at her hands, already glowing with her powers. She is stronger than I've ever seen her. I can't even imagine how much more she would be if not for Joachim's stupidity. If all four of us had fulfilled our duties to her, she might not even need us to protect her from Nergal any longer. She certainly could take out Rasputin like a bug under her shoe.

The dragon warrior glares at me. "My brethren recognize the goddess's gift of my freedom as our one true hope of breaking Ereshkigal's curse on us. We've got centuries of experience in deflecting Nergal's commands."

Taryn eyes the dragon warrior. "I think I need to have a chat with Ereshkigal."

I imagine a conversation between the Goddess of the Moon and the Goddess of the Underworld would be... illuminating. "Let's work on getting rid of her consort first. We've seen Nergal's attack patterns twice now, and I suspect they're being directed by Rasputin. We lay a trap with your portals, sending Nergal back to Hell, and capture Rasputin so we can break our own curse."

The dragon warrior points toward the nearest treeline. "You don't have time for plans or traps, your enemy is at the gates."

We all turn to see what he's indicating. Yep. There's Rasputin coming out of the treeline, with Nergal flying figure eights in the sky overhead. Behind them the animal eyes of dozens of wolves blink in the brush and trees like lightning bugs.

Rasputin has brought reinforcements. I should have killed him already and not given him the chance to call up an army to hide behind. He'll be harder to get to now and that makes Taryn more vulnerable. But I must trust that she is the powerful warrior woman I love.

"Ready, my queen? Looks like we've got a shit load of Volkovs to send to Hell."

She narrows her eyes and I see her own wolf rising up, ready to defend her pack with the ferocity of a wolftress who's been wronged. "No, but let's do this anyway."

Taryn touches August, me, and Vas, shooting a warm bolt of her magic inside of us, giving us a layer of protection. We three form a phalanx in front of her and with her at our backs, we step forward and onto the field of battle.

If it is for the last time, I will haunt Joachim in this life and the next and the next.

JOACHIM

I drop to my knees and bow my head. I've spent an eternity like this in prayer, to my goddess or someone else's god trying so hard to will my trespasses away. I know the sins I've committed. August, Vasily, and Grigori's disappointment in me isn't unexpected. Their condemnation is not any worse than my own.

But somewhere buried deep in my heart was the stupid hope that my goddess would forgive me. She shouldn't. I didn't even expect her to.

I am still crushed.

The prayer beads click and clack as they run through my fingers. I'm not speaking the incantations nor even thinking them to myself. The motions themselves soothe me and the moment I realize that, I stop. I deserve a good flagellation, self-inflicted or even better a lashing from my Goddess. Something, anything other than this devastating withdrawal of her love.

As if in a vision from God, I know what to do. I can't let Rasputin have a hold on Taryn's magic for another moment longer. I either must kill him or be killed. But reclaiming the magic I gave to him will destroy every single thing about our world, and I'm not ready to lose her forever.

I get to my feet and throw off my robes. For far too long I've suppressed my wolf because when I do, the base feelings I can't control are also buried. Today I can let all my rage run wild. I can face the sacrifices I know I must make but am still unsure of.

My bones break and reform, claws burst out from beneath my fingernails, my skin splits and the fur pushes out, my fangs push my other teeth aside and burst through my gums, and I let the wildness overtake me.

I will end Rasputin. The island will claim his body, and may his soul be a snack for Ereshkigal.

I scratch at the door, ready to break it down, but Maggie opens it and gives me a disapproving look I don't have the capacity to interpret right now. Am I repeating the same mistake again?

Taryn hates me not for my mistake in giving her power over to the Volkovs, but for making the decision to do so on my own. I can't and won't ask her or Grigori's permission. Not for this. Because they'll say no.

I must repent.

The battle has already begun. Taryn's put up a shield around her heart that sends a chill up and down my spine. Her love for me is there, but it's as if it's covered in the same frigid snow that has covered the ground on this forsaken island for so long. Until she came and warmed all of us up with her love.

My mistakes can't be the reason she gets hurt in this battle or gets stuck here for the rest of eternity. I have known since I first felt her magic come through my prayer beads months ago, that this was our one and only chance to all be together once again.

I fucking tried to get the rest of them to come to the first mating ceremony and we all could have joined with our Goddess once again. Then she wouldn't have found out about what I'd done and we'd all be safe and wrapped up in her warm love and body once again.

But no. They had to have their little pouts and... I'm being the ultimate asshole once again, deflecting my pain onto the brethren I trust in above all else. What the fuck is wrong with me? When did I become worse than a man like Rasputin, self serving, and narcissistic?

I will repent, I will sacrifice everything I am, and I will not disappoint Taryn or the rest of her Wolf Guard again.

I run toward the battle already in progress. The wolves of the *derevnya* have joined the phalanx that August, Vas, and Grigori have formed in front of Taryn. I'm sure it's driving Grigori mad that she's putting herself in the center of the fight, but maybe he's finally learned to trust that she knows herself and her abilities.

Taryn is opening portals that still look like they lead only to Hell. But our new ally, the black dragon, Jett, is flicking in and out of them, using his own power over shadow, and that must be why no new demon wyrms are joining the fray. It's just the Volkovs against the prisoners.

Rasputin sends a small pack straight for Taryn and her guards and it kills me not to rush to their assistance. Vas quickly dispatches the first two, and August rips the head off another. We were all trained to fight by Grigori and there's no one better to keep her safe.

Except maybe Taryn herself. I stumble when I look up to see Nergal, wings tucked in, dive bombing my *boginya* herself. Before I can even react, she's shot her magic into the sky and opened a handful of portals, creating an obstacle course that even the God of Chaos can't navigate safely.

Although, he should be able to. His connection with Rasputin has weakened him and Grigori is smart to take advantage of that mistake.

With all this activity, no one notices me moving to the front line. Good. I don't need any grief from Grigori for doing my sworn duty. I will protect my Goddess whether any of them want me to or not. This gives me the leeway to hunt for Rasputin.

Since I'm clearly not needed there, I continue to push my way forward through the gathered ranks. I itch to stop and give platitudes and prayers to those in line for battle, but I am no longer a spiritual advisor for her people. That is no longer my path.

I will destroy the prayer beads he possesses that hold that portion of Taryn's power. She may never forgive me, never claim me or allow me to claim her, but hopefully the magic Rasputin possesses will be enough to boost hers to the point where she can free her people.

That is a cause I can be worthy of. I will save her so that she may save others.

"What exactly do you think you're doing, Father?" Taryn's voice pops into my head and I stumble for a second time. She may not trust or love me any longer, but our connection hasn't been severed and that gives me hope.

By the time I regain my footing I've formulated my response. *"My duty,* boygina.*"*

I finally make it to the front line and I'm happy to release the guilt and anger pulsing through me on those who would serve the despotic Volkovs. Two wolves come at me, and I swipe at one with my claws and snap at the other. I am twice as big as they are and better trained. With only a bit of effort, their blood pools at my feet and the island absorbs their bodies. *"May the Goddess bless you with the ability to choose the right side in your next life."*

August and Vas leave a trail of blood and destruction in their wake too. Yet somehow the Volkovs keep coming. How many souls has Rasputin corrupted in the years I've been imprisoned? Without her guards to find her and help her rise to power in wolf society, Taryn must not have been able to influence the wolf tzars. We haven't had enough new prisoners to the island with news of the outside world to understand the current political situation.

And Rasputin has definitely taken advantage of our absence. Even if I die this day in my mission to get those cursed prayer beads from him, it will not be in vain if Taryn can rule once again over our people. Because there is no way she will allow this piece of trash to control the lives of those she holds most dear.

I tear through another swath of Volkovs and like the progress I'm making toward Rasputin's position. His forces and attention are torn between holding back the Wolf Guard and me. The closer I get, the more I can see he's also struggling to control Nergal. His own goddess doesn't favor him quite enough to give him total control over her consort. That is a strategic mistake on his part.

One of desperation.

He knows his reign is coming to an end.

I'll be the one to end it.

"Stand down, Guard of the House of the Divided Moon." Grigori's demands are easy to ignore as long as he doesn't use his alpha voice on me. I've been neglecting what he wants for thousands of years, mostly because he trusted me, and didn't know to command me to bare my transgressions for all to see.

"Only she can take away the responsibility I bear in service to her, Alpha." I'm not even sure if he did use his all powerful alpha voice on me it would negate that calling.

Vas growls into my head. *"You're a distraction and that's going to get someone killed."*

Even as he says it, he smashes two Volkovs into the trees so hard I can hear the wood and their bones break from way the hell over here. I'm so close to Rasputin, I can see the wolf shining in his eyes. He hasn't shifted and is vulnerable. This is my chance. *"Then stop talking to me and treat me like any other wolf out here fighting for our Goddess."*

I feel Taryn's frustrated sigh at my rebuttal all the way to my broken heart. *"But you're not any other wolf. You're mine and I'm tired of fighting."*

That halts all four of us in our tracks. Something has changed in her tone and her demeanor. Is she giving up? That's not what I want. *"Boginya?"*

She doesn't answer and from my position, I see the blue glow of her magic is spreading out around her and absorbing all those around her like a shield. Rasputin finally shifts and the beads around his neck glow with the same light of her power.

It's not a shield, but a beacon, one where she is at the center. Nergal screeches right above my head and dives, his talons outstretched. Grigori, August, and Vas spin to face her in a panic and move to cover her, but they aren't going to be fast enough.

Everyone is racing toward her and time around us slows until only my Goddess is at normal speed. She walks through the wolves frozen in battle, toward me. The air around me shimmers, and I blink through a fog that's covered my eyes. Have I been killed in the fight by some rogue Volkov? I must be dead and she's coming to claim my soul after all.

Except August falls in line behind her, he too stalks toward me. I know he hasn't been killed, I would have seen it happen. Then Vas joins, and finally Grigori. The glow of her magic surrounds them too, and we are all under her spell.

They surround me and Taryn cups my jaw. In that brief moment I am not a wolf, I am not a man. I am both and I am neither. I am only what she wants me to be. I lean into her touch and, for the first time in as long as I can remember, I give myself permission to revel in her physical affection.

The heat of her touch intensifies as if she was summer itself. *"Don't you see the magic in all of us together? This only works when I have all of my guards, and they have me."*

I close my eyes and wish away the last five thousand years where I lived the very embodiment of sin against her. *"I know."*

"Then why do you continue to hold yourself apart?" She pulls me to her chest and strokes my hair as she would if we'd just made love and weren't ready to let go of each other. But these are not sweet nothings she's whispering to me, but condemnations of my entire existence.

"You don't want me anymore." A shiver takes over my entire body and I almost cry out from the chill of it. I try to pull away, but Taryn doesn't let me go.

"What I want is for you to give yourself over to me as you once did so long ago. When did you stop trusting in me, in us?"

"*I...*" I'm about to say I haven't, but isn't that what's got me into this mess in the first place? I didn't trust her to know whether we four guards were enough to keep her safe in those early days when she was so weak. I didn't trust Grigori, August, and Vas to be smart enough, strategic enough, to even consult with my plan.

I still didn't trust them. No, no, that couldn't be right. I trusted all of them with my very life. There was something deeper inside that kept me from sharing what I knew to be the right thing to do. I was afraid.

Of what, I don't know. Probably because I've been fobbing those fears off on my spirituality and religion. It was a convenient and easy place to hide it away.

She trusted me to be her spiritual advisor in life after life, when really she was mine. I wanted to feel all of that again. To do that I have to let all four of them back into my life.

All of it.

The moment I make that decision, the world snaps back to the frenzied fray of the battle. I'm still near Rasputin, and Taryn and the rest of the Guard are in the heat of their part of the fight.

The only clue I have that anything happened is the fact that Nergal is still dive bombing toward her, and she's looking directly at me.

If I hurry I can use the outcropping of rock ahead of me to catapult into the air and stop Nergal's attack. He can't be allowed to touch her. But if I do, I move away from Rasputin and the prayer beads holding her captive.

I don't know the right path.

I don't know.

Now is the time to let go of my fears and trust my beloved and my brethren with not only my life, but with their own.

TARYN

Whoa. I had no idea I could do any of that. I'm not even sure I know what I just did. I was in Joachim's mind... or his consciousness... or his soul. Whatever or wherever I was, we were so intimately connected that I can still feel every single one of his emotions.

It's similar to how August, Vasily, and Grigori felt to me when we mated. But that settled into a softer but constant connection. Somehow this new link I have with Joachim feels like it's always been there. It even makes my connections with the other guards feel older too.

I wish I could make it happen again, but I'm not even sure what I did in the first place. I sensed what he was doing even though he's still trying to keep it from us. I won't let him sacrifice himself. He can't die on me now.

Am I mad at him, sure. Can I see the two of us getting naked and intimate with each other? I've been fantasizing about that even when I thought it was completely inappropriate. I'll never give up that need I have for him. I just need some time to work through these feelings.

But in that moment, I was simply desperate for him to be with us, no longer separate. I don't feel whole without him. None of us do. Just because we're hurt doesn't mean we don't still love him.

There's a shift in his mind now, and we can all feel it. He's letting us in. Thank God. Oops. Uh, I mean, thank Goddess? I'm gonna need some new vernacular when this is all over. Let's go with thank the Universe for right now.

"Boginya, we must get to Rasputin." He wasn't only projecting his thoughts to me, but to August, Vasily, and Grigori too. What he is saying isn't a demand. My heart melts a little because despite his open and fresh emotional wounds, he is trying to reconnect.

"No shit. What do you think we're trying to do." Grigori snaps and the tension between them pings like an off key set of bagpipes. While I'm working on forgiving Father Joachim, Grigori isn't quite there yet. I get it, I do. The wounds are fresh, and Grigori isn't made for forgiveness. It's going to take him a long time.

I simply want us to have that time, and Joachim going off and getting himself killed isn't the way.

Guilt pervades our connection and while I don't like it, Joachim needs to work through it. His mistakes aren't just something any of us can just brush off. *"I'm trying to learn from my past mistakes and not simply act on what I think is the right thing to do."*

That's what I like to hear and I want to run over and snuggle him right in the face and see his tail wag. Which is slightly ridiculous because he's a six foot tall werewolf and not a puppy. I'm just so tickled that he listened and is trying to work on his shit.

Any other day and we'd be making our way to the church in the forest so we could claim each other. Maybe I'm being too forgiving, but while I was hurt, I still believe in the power of us all being together. I'll be mad for a while, but just because I'm pissed doesn't mean we aren't going to save the world.

Or at least this island and all my people who've been trapped here.*"You're right, August. That's not the real problem. I can get to Rasputin, but what we really need are those prayer beads. Only that can break this curse. But I don't know that I can survive."*

Well, God dammit. Sorry Father.

Break the curse so that this half existence we've been living finally ends, but not be able to be the Goddess I truly am or save the last of my beloved guards so that I can once again ascend? To me there is no question. I will not lose Joachim.

As I'm trying to prove to them all, it's not only my choice. But I do get a say. If I say it now, it may sway the others. "This isn't exactly a great time for a meeting. Can this be an email?"

"If an email is a death spell, then yes, this should be an email."

Oops. Sometimes I forget that my guards have been

imprisoned without the modern technologies of man for a hundred or more years. It's gonna be fun to reintroduce them to my world. Because we are getting out of here. I will reclaim my power and then Rasputin and Nergal are going down. Literally. Hell has their name on it.

Nergal swoops down again, but I've got his attack pattern down pat now. Or rather, I've got Rasputin's because I'm more sure with every passing moment Nergal is going to break free of the Volkov's compulsion over him, and then we're all in a lot more trouble. Rasputin is predictable. The God of Chaos, not so much. I throw up another series of portals and he can't get to us. I wish he'd just miss and go popping off back to Hell. I'm so telling on him to Ereshkigal.

How in the world did she ever let Rasputin have such free rein on her powers? Now that I know what he is, I can smell her on him. The Queen of the Underworld has a certain scent of death about her. No wonder I've been repulsed by the Volkovs. Not that worshiping a goddess is bad. They can venerate who they want. This is something wrong. They are my people and I'm not a fan of sharing.

If they left me of their own free will, fine. But that scent of death on them is unnatural. Missing pieces of my current life snap into place. I'm letting the Volkov minions off too easily. These wolves are who the Troikas were fighting against. The one-bloods.

They chose to leave me.

Because I wasn't there for them? My people have lived in fear, and that's the opposite of why I gave them the gift of shifting into powerful beasts. I see everything in my past through a dual lens now. That of the wolftress who's lived a thousand lives and seen the evolution of life without the guidance of a goddess, and that goddess herself, imprisoned, unable to help her own people.

I understand better and remember more about how they've been the ones to manipulate my lives. I remember Rasputin being around me as a young child more often than not. He influenced my parents, my life, and the lives of my guards to make sure I couldn't remember who or what I truly was. I doubt if Ereshkigal even understands what kind of liberties he's taken with her powers here on the Earthly realm.

He is the epitome of the modern day one-bloods. Greed and power, to the point of corruption over all else. Why did he choose to worship the Queen of the Underworld instead of the Goddess of the Moon?

My sweet August is the first of the protectors to let down his guard. *"Of course you should attack Rasputin. That's not really a question, is it? Try again, dickhead."*

Okay, maybe August isn't ready to let Joachim back in either.

Several more wolves attack us, but at this point, I'm not sure why Rasputin keeps sending them our way. None have even gotten close to me. A few have torn some bits off my guards though. It's as if they aren't even trying to get to me.

Gasp. Shit. Whooo boy. They aren't. Dammit. Why didn't I see it earlier? Rasputin wants my guards dead because without all four of them, I can't get back my full powers. He won't hurt me if he can help it, but he'll sure as shit hurt my men.

"You're right, August. That's not the real problem. I can get to Rasputin, but what we really need are those prayer beads. Only that can break this curse. But I don't know that I can survive."

Well, God dammit. Sorry Father. Joachim wants to redeem himself. I don't like his whole sacrificial vibe, and no way we're losing him when we're so damn close to being one heart, one soul once again. *"No, Father, wait. It's better if we all attack together."*

I don't know how but Nergal reacts to what I'm saying and changes his tactics. He swoops up into a wide loop, avoiding all my portals to Hell and aims his talons right for Father Joachim. Rasputin cackles in the back of my mind and I brush my hair and skin as if I can wipe him away like a bug.

"Get out of my head you dickmunch eye of a potato." I bring up a bolt of blue magic and pull my arm back to give it my all and throw it directly at Rasputin or Nergal, or both. Argh, can I make this two birds and one stone?

I hurl what I've got and Grigori jumps directly in front of my missle of magic. Shit. Shit. Shit. I make a fist to try and pull the spell I've thrown in anger. It still glances off Grigori's haunches and I close my eyes and scream.

I can't look. What if I sent his lower half to Hell, or turned his butt human and nothing else. Oh no... human bits are so much more vulnerable. If I've killed him by exposing him from the waist down, I'll die and then die again.

Grigori makes an ooph sound and I can't take it. I have to see what I've done. I expect his ass to be on fire at the least, but it's not. He's been propelled by my magic like a freaking firecracker. He barrels through a whole swath of bad guy wolves and runs right into Rasputin.

They tumble claws over ass, and that's the exact moment Nergal breaks whatever bond Rasputin has over him. He dives directly toward me and I shoot out a hundred portals, but just as I predicted, there's nothing stopping him this time. His razor sharp talons are about a foot in front of my face and I drop to the ground and roll away.

August's body slams into the owl's body and Vasily sinks his teeth into a wing. Nergal squawks, but tosses them both aside. Without Rasputin hindering him, he's much more powerful. Grigori and Joachim come rushing toward us, but with one big flap of his wings, Nergal blows Grigori halfway across the town and he goes crashing into the barn.

Rasputin pulls out the prayer beads that we have to get to break the curse and crushes them in his hand. They glow with a blue-black hue and Joachim falls as if he's been shot, skidding across the ground, hitting Rasputin and knocking him down.

Aw, hell no. Nobody hurts my wolves. I jump up and explode with power. My magical blue light pours out from everywhere and I am going to fuck this guy up with my magic god-damned vagina if I have to.

Sorry Father.

I am all fired up and quite literally using my rage as rocket fuel. I fly up into the air, just a foot or so feeling like SuperGirl or Wonder Woman. I shoot a bolt of blue magic at the approaching asshat birdman. Nergal screeches, but flounders and my shot misses him. Crap.

Rasputin is back on his feet and is chanting some kind of incantation. His eyes are rolled back in his head and Father Joachim lays at his feet unmoving. That fucking bastard. Rasputin, not Joachim. Although, if my sweet priest has died before we can be mated, I'm going to kill him.

Maybe it's time one of us grabbed those cursed beads off Rasputin.

Joachim can't be dead. I can still feel his soul reaching out for mine, and the island hasn't taken his body. He is injured though and his wolf needs time to heal him. I search for anyone that can run interference. Grigori is rushing back through the *derevnya* with Will right on his heels, but they're so far away. August is fighting his way through a gauntlet of Volkovs, but more keep coming. I hear Vas's howl and see him scrambling through his own battles to get back here.

It's got to be up to me

We should have just let Joachim attack Rasputin when he wanted to. It was a good plan. There's always risk involved when it comes to fighting evil. I don't know that he was really going to sacrifice himself just to break the spell.

Now he's hurt and none of us are close enough to save him.

"Joachim, don't you dare die on me. Get up and fight. For me, fight for me." Even if he can't move, I will fight for him. If he dies without knowing how much I love him, I will never recover.

With every bit of my power I can muster, I speed toward Rasputin, feeling more magic building up inside of me. I don't know what's in those beads he's got, but they are mine, dammit. They're. Mine.

Grigori, Will, August, Vasily, and I are all rushing toward Rasputin, and converging with us is that flying rat eater Nergal. I won't use my magic willy nilly, I've learned the consequences too many times. So that just means I have to get to Joachim faster.

I'm a breath away from him when he opens his eyes and relief pours through me like a hot toddy. But like the drink, it burns a moment later when his eyes go wide. I know Nergal is right behind me. I won't take the effort to look because it will take away from the power I'm using to hurry to get to Joachim.

Rasputin cackles and his eyes go white like a fucking zombie. Nergal screeches and sinks his talons into my back, piercing me all the way through my shoulders and chest. Blue light shoots out of my wounds and into my four wolves.

Joachim receives the full force of it first and his eyes,

claws, and fangs glow with my magic as if he's a radioactive werewolf. He pounces on Rasputin, crushing him into the dirt, sending the prayer beads flying. He uses Rasputin's spine as a springboard to jump into the air and crashes into Nergal, sending all three of us crashing to the ground.

Just as we hit the Earth below us, I catch the prayer beads and clutch them to my chest. When I smash into the ground, it knocks the air clean out of me and I'm dazed, my ears ringing, and I taste the blood bubbling up my throat.

I roll and cry out with pain. Not because of my own injuries, but because lying next to me is Father Joachim, the severed talon of the God of Chaos through his chest. No light is in his eyes, no soul left in his body.

He's dead, and the island is taking his body right before my eyes.

JOACHIM

God dammit. Yeah. This is bad enough that I very willfully will take the Lord's name in vain. He's not my lord anyway. I don't have a lord, but a lady, and I've lost her.

How?

I'm dead.

How the fuck am I dead? Again.

Wherever I am is not the underworld. Am I in some kind of purgatory? Has the Christian God I adopted laid me on his altar to be weighed and measured? He'd most certainly send me to Hell for my sins against him and my own Goddess.

Taryn.

My beautiful *boginya*.

My mind is fuzzy but I'm sure I saw those fucking prayer beads in her hand. The curse is broken. She will be free. Only in that knowledge can I find any respite.

I deserve to die for all the ways I've wronged her. Even in the end she loved me, and what did I do for her but fuck up her life?

So many regrets circle me like vultures waiting for my body to rot in my grief. This death is so unlike the thousands of others. I know this time, I won't be reincarnated. There is no second, third, four-thousandth chance with her.

"Phew. This one sti-inks. Are you sure we're supposed to be here?"

At least I know she is strong. She's almost regained all her powers and with the curse broken, perhaps she will still be able to find a way to lead her people off the island.

"Yes, my love. I'm sure. Just keep your voice down. We don't need Ereshkigal or anyone else getting wind that we're interfering with one of my mother's people."

I would so like to be able to have seen her ascend...

"Aha. I knew it. We aren't allowed here. I shall be as stealthy as a super secret sneaky spy."

Who or what keeps invading my melancholy memories of my final life. "Do you mind? I am trying to wallow in my grief and remember those I've left behind."

"Oooh, he's feisty." The deep rumbling male voice is getting closer, and I wonder if this is one of Ereshkigal's annunaki come to drag me off to her domain. Somehow I assumed they'd be a bit more reverential to the dead. This demon or whatever it is has a distinct flippancy that I

don't like. "A spicy, salty *douchepotato. Shall I knock him around a bit? Show him who's boss?"*

"*Kur.*" The female voice sounds as irritated with her partner as I am. Perhaps she is the true annunaki and this other one is... her pet. "*We need him to do our bidding, so perhaps a more gentle approach is called for.*"

Their bidding? Shit. Is this my penance for a life of sin? I'm to become a demon and wreak havoc on the unsuspecting? That would be my hell, indeed.

I have no sense of my body or I would get up and have a look around. I doubt there is any avoiding the fate of my afterlife, but then again, August and Vas survived what must have seemed like an eternity in Hell. Not that there will be any escape for me.

Since I don't seem to have an actual body, I instinctively reach for my wolf and am surprised to find the spirit of my beast ready and prepared to act. The wolf is ruffled by these strange visitors, but isn't afraid. More like irritated by their presence. I reach out with my senses and scent... a dragon?

What. The. Fuck?

No, I must be wrong. Perhaps it's a demon dragon like Jett. Even with the darkness in his soul, he wasn't evil. But as I expand my senses to understand who and what is here with me, I feel only a mix of emotions including grief, but also hopefulness.

A bright white presence appears before me and I'm overwhelmed by her beauty. A soft, plump woman with dark olivey skin and a radiance so like that of my own

Goddess appears before me. Robes of white decorated with prismatic rainbows sparkle all around her and if I could, I would bow and genuflect before her.

Because I know exactly who this is.

"Inanna, Goddess of Love. I would bow before you if I could. I am overwhelmed by your favor." Perhaps I wasn't destined for Hell after all. She was the goddess associated with heaven back when I was little more than a young man in what was now an ancient civilization.

"Ooh, we've got ourselves a smarty-smart pants over here. Don't forget the part about being the Goddess of Beauty, Sex, Fertility, War, Justice, Political Power, and Prostitutes too." The male voice hovers around us like an irritating fly. Fucking dragons. *"Oh, and my very luscious mate, thank you very much."*

"Yes, of course, my lady of many domains." But she was not my goddess. Not the one I chose to worship, not the one I'd betrayed. "But why do you seek me out? I am—"

"Yes, I know who you are, En of Ningal, Guardian of the House of Divided Moon. That is why I am here. I need you to give my mother something that will... well, that's all very complicated. But when you wake up, please give this to Taryn. She'll know what to do with it."

Wake up? I'm not asleep, I'm dead.

The dragon finally appears before me and shifts into a human form. He slaps me on the shoulder, which I wasn't aware I even had until he touched me. He leans in to say something to me, as if to share a secret. *"And get your shit together, wolf. Goddesses don't like to be kept waiting. Especially not for their orgasms."*

"What?" I got no answer. What I did get is a sensation like a thousand knives stabbing me from the inside, while from the outside I'm being snuggled by a hundred and one fluffy kittens. The discordant sensations push my mind and body into overdrive. Utter and complete sadness tears me apart, while the most intense joy puts me back together again, but not as I was before. I am young and untried, I am thousands of years old and tired, so tired.

I am earth, I am wind, water flows through me, over me baptizing me anew. Fire and brimstone burn me back up again.

Death consumes me, and then...

I gasp and sit bolt upright. My ears are ringing, my vision is fuzzy and it hurts to blink. My lungs burn, but I find the strength to croak out just one singular word. "Taryn."

A soft cool hand touches my forehead and gently pushes me back down to a prone position. I don't have the strength to resist but I do say her name again. "Taryn."

"I'm right here, *dusha moya.*" I blink, but still can't focus to see her. "Quiet now, you've been through hell and it's going to take a minute to recover.

"I wasn't in Hell. I don't know where I was." I try to recall what just happened to me, but like a dream, the memory is fading faster than I can grab onto it. Something about a white light, a mother, and some kind of rainbows? None of it makes a lick of sense.

Taryn's face starts to come into focus, and as my vision clears I see Maggie and Will beside her. Another couple of blinks and Grigori, August, and Vas come into view too. Grigori is glaring at me, August is swiping his tongue across his fangs like he's going to eat me, and Vas is smacking his fist against his open palm.

I may have just been resurrected, but I think I'm about to get my ass kicked. Until Taryn holds up her hand and the three of them sag. "I can feel the anger rolling off the three of you. Knock it off. You can kill him again later after we've mated."

Mated? Uh. I think I'm feeling better already. In fact, I feel some blood pumping through my veins and most of it is going down below my belt. I open my mouth and close it again, not knowing what to say. I'm not worthy of my Goddess or her forgiveness.

"You don't think you're going to put me off again, do you, Joachim? Your vows to the Christian God can't possibly be as sacred as your one to me, can it?"

Fuck. "I never should have hidden behind the chastity of priesthood. I… I needed something to believe in when I thought I'd failed you."

"You're a dumbshit," Grigori calls from behind Taryn.

Yes. I am. A douchepotato even. I don't exactly know what that is, but I assume it's much worse and I'm deserving of it.

Taryn runs the back of her fingers over my cheek and

across my jaw. "They're not wrong, but that doesn't mean I didn't die a whole lot when you did."

Oh goddess. I did die. I wasn't entirely sure, because, how does one recover from death if not by reincarnation. When she has her full powers, even my Goddess can't bring people back from the dead. "But how? What happened?"

I sit up, despite Taryn's hand on my shoulder. We're in Will and Maggie's barn and there are a few other wolves laid out on makeshift beds suffering from battle wounds. None are in any desperate condition and our wolves' supernatural healing abilities will take care of them. A day ago I would set aside my own injuries and help tend to them. I no longer feel qualified to help anyone.

I am not the same man, or even the same wolf as I was even an hour ago. I have been reborn and can't make the same mistakes of my past with this second chance.

Taryn slides her hand into mine and for the first time, I notice her tear stained face. She swallows and shakes her head, then looks to Grigori. He steps forward and caresses her hair, giving her comfort. My own hands tingle with wanting to do the same, but it is because of me that she needs soothing in the first place.

Grigori takes a deep breath and he's either about to berate me or—

"You don't even know what you gave Rasputin when you made that cursed deal, do you?"

Okay, a tongue-lashing it is. Even I know dying for my sins isn't enough penance. But Taryn gives my hand a squeeze and for the first time, I don't feel as though I need to be punished anymore. "I do. My mistake was not in hiding her magic from Nergal, but in not trusting the rest of you. I will use the rest of my existence working to repair the harm I've done to our relationship, but I won't apologize again for giving Rasputin a piece of Taryn's magic. It saved her, and it saved us until she could be strong enough to defend herself once again."

A tear drips down Taryn's cheek and I swipe at it with my thumb. "No more tears, *boginya.* We'll get through this together."

She nods but a few more tears escape. "Yeah, we will, now that we have you back for real."

I don't understand what that means. I look to Grigori and he glares at me. That's going to be a long road to regain his trust. I'm willing to walk it. For all of them. "You didn't give Rasputin her magic. You gave him the ability to reincarnate us when and where he liked, to track her and all of us in each of those lives, and manipulate us all."

"But he hid her and us from Nergal. How could he do that without her magic?" I put almost everything I had into those prayer beads, keeping only my connection to her in my own.

"You're the dumbest smart guy I've ever known. Rasputin was and is a priest of the cult of Ereshkigal. They deal in life and death, not magic. They deal in souls."

Taryn lifts her hand from mine and I see my prayer beads wrapped around her wrist. But not just mine. The ones I gave to Rasputin as well. The two strands were intertwined becoming whole once again. I knew she'd be able to break the curse when she got them back. So what was I missing?

She unwinds the beads and dangles them between us. They're glowing with her pure moonlight as if her very essence is inside. "The prayer beads you were so careful to cherish held that bit of magic I shared with you when we claimed each other and mated that first time. That can't ever be taken away. Ever."

Oh holy Goddess. I have no words. Her love is so all encompassing and I'm basking in it, undeserved or not. I belong to her and always will. Always.

"What you gave Rasputin was the bond not only between you and me, but with August, Vas, and Grigori. What you gave him was your soul." As she says these heaven and earth-shattering words, Taryn shoves the beads directly into my chest and I'm literally filled with a sense of awe, wonder, love, and finally, finally, peace.

Everyone is staring at me, and I don't care about anything but the beautiful goddess who has saved me. I reach out and slide my hands into her hair. For so long I've denied myself anything that was good and right because I felt so unworthy.

No more.

I look her directly in the eyes and it takes me a moment to find the words, I'm so lost in her. "I am yours, if you'll have me."

For the first time since I reawoke, she smiles and gives

me a slow nod. There are new tears in her eyes, but these ones aren't sad. I kiss one, tasting the tang of her joy, then another, and another. With my brethren as my witnesses, I press my lips to hers and kiss her. Kiss her like there's no tomorrow and let the magic of loving her break free from my hardened heart. "I, Joachim, Guard of the House of the Divided Moon, claim you, Taryn, my Goddess, as my own."

TARYN

*J*oachim is finally mine.

I mean, he always was, but now he understands. Hallelujah.

Too bad it took him dying to figure it out. I despise Rasputin with all of my being, but if he hadn't been keeping Joachim's soul in those damn prayer beads, I would have lost him forever. Holding his soul in my hands was the most spiritual experience of my existence. I will forever be awed by everything he's sacrificed for me.

I would not have been able to call him back from dead without the deep connection the five of us have. Even through their anger at him, August, Vasily, and Grigori joined hearts and minds with me and only together were we able to give him renewed life. It's brought us all even closer together and I know the rest of the guard are anxious for Joachim and I to finally mate so we can all feel whole again.

With his soul restored, I have before me the real Joachim. The one I fell in love with so many moons ago. I find myself strangely nervous now. It's not because Nergal is still on the loose, nor the fact that I'm about to be able to fully ascend into my true goddess state.

I know what will happen afterwards. I've got a plan. But Joachim has denied us both the connection of claiming and mating for several lifetimes. This one is special, and I want it to be just right, and I'm afraid that can't happen. I always did enjoy the ritualistic part of worship and religion. Especially when they worshiped me.

The cults of the Sumerian gods and goddesses are all long gone, and I don't really care. Tonight I only want to be worshiped by one man. Well... maybe a few more. I need to claim and be claimed by Joachim. He and I will mate. But this will also be the first opportunity to be with all my guards, all my lovers, at once for the first time in five thousand years.

I didn't realize how alone I've felt without them all by my side and in my heart until right now.

A rattling and shouts come from the far side of the barn. "It will never work, you stupid beasts. Nergal will destroy her and then there won't be anything stopping me from ruling the wolves the way they should be."

All eyes turn to the weak and now frail man Rasputin has become. He turned out to be incredibly hard to kill.

Without Joachim's soul connecting him to the five of us, all he has fueling him now is Ereshkigal's gifts and bitter rage.

Vasily takes a few steps over and punches him in the face. "Shut the fuck up."

I'd snicker if it wasn't so sad. Once upon a time, this man was one of my people. He gave that all up for greed and power, for control. It's disgusting and I've had enough. I stand and have to push both August and Grigori out of my way to get to where we have Rasputin chained up in the corner.

"Why did you forsake me for Ereshkigal, Rasputin?" His answer doesn't matter, I merely want him to have to think about what he's done before he feels the consequences of his choices.

He snarls at me as if he's feral. I know better. He's scared. I wait in silence and he can't stand it. "You chose your favorites and the rest of us were left with nothing but your curse."

Vasily cracks Rasputin in the face again. "The Goddess gave us a gift that you've manipulated and squandered, you fool."

"There's no power in being hunted by humankind and having to hide from the world when we should be masters over them all." There's no wolf in his eyes where there should be, and that's sad. He's suppressed that part of his nature with his hate and shame. "Being a slathering beast, a monster who cares only about finding and fucking a mate is no gift."

"Watch your mouth." Vas punches Rasputin so hard this time, I hear his jaw crack. His wolf will be able to heal it quickly.

Joachim joins us, moving tenderly, as his own wounds are still healing. He should shift and let his own wolf finish healing him. I hate to see him suffering. I hate to see any of my people in pain. "You've never understood the gift for what it is. You wanted power, when what she offered us was so much more."

"There was no offer. I never wanted this." Rasputin jerks against the restraints. "One day I was a man and the next an abomination."

Huh. I only offered that piece of myself, my magic and the ability to shift, to those who worshiped at my altar. He absolutely was one of my people, so how did it all go so wrong with him?

"I ask you again, Rasputin. Why did you forsake me?" I thought my memories were completely restored, but I have no clue why Rasputin hates me or being a wolf shifter so much. This is one of the last mysteries left by the holes in my formerly Swiss cheese brain. Or perhaps is something I was never privy to in the first place.

"You're the one who rejected me, you fickle goddess." Rasputin spits at me, but Joachim moves so the spittle strikes him instead of me.

"She didn't, I did." Grigori doesn't move from his spot, but that tenor of power resonates throughout the whole room. "You were not worthy of her then, and you aren't now."

"I would have been a better choice than this fool who literally gave up his soul and then killed her by his own hand." Rasputin jerks his chin at Joachim. "Did you really think that would keep her safe?"

That is apparently all August can take of Rasputin, because he's the one who punches him this time. "You didn't get chosen to be one of her guards so you made a deal with demons? Tell me again who the fool is."

"Dumuzid offered me a hell of a lot more if I worshiped Ereshkigal than any of you ever did. Look at the last five centuries. Who has been at the core of our society, manipulating all the pieces just so. Me. While you all just scrambled about trying to get your dicks sucked."

Dumuzid? The same Dumuzid who betrayed my daughter Inanna?

Wait. Holy shit.

It is well past time I get all my damned memory back and reassume my throne in the heavens because I am tired of memories just popping up like burnt fucking Pop-Tarts. I have two daughters and a son. I had a husband who was also a god. Where the fuck is he?

I want like five billion years of back child support.

Although, I guess I've been a bit of an absentee mother. I'll have to work on that later. Right now I'm going to set a few things straight.

Both Vasily and August are winding up again to beat Rasputin, and while he deserves to be a pile of pulp, I'm going to do them one better. "Gentleman, allow me."

They step aside and I press my fingers to Rasputin's

forehead. I see all of his memories. All. Of. Them. He deserves much worse than what I'm going to do to him and I've got some new to-dos on my list for once we get back to the real world. "I rescind my gift to you and denounce you as one of my people. Never more shall you bask in the light of my glory. Let the darkness in your soul be no solace to you until Ereshkigal reclaims your life and you serve her in the Underworld for eternity."

The spirit of a wolf, battered and sad, rises up from the place where I'm touching Rasputin's head and howls with an eerie mournful bay. I release the poor spirit and its light shimmers and fades away.

Rasputin collapses, his body withering before our eyes. He has only whatever offerings he received from Dumuzid or Ereshkigal left to sustain him. He won't perish here and now, but it won't be long before the Anunnaki come to claim his soul. Good riddance.

But with this severance, I can also see the tether that Rasputin has held over Nergal slip away. I listen for his tell-tale screech, but none sounds. I doubt we have very long before he attacks once again, but of course he'll wait until the most chaotic time to launch against me.

Which probably means right when I'm mating with Joachim.

Fuck him. I'm not waiting another minute to claim my mate. Not one more minute.

I spin around and find exactly who I'm looking for standing there waiting for me. "Maggie, Will, I hate to ask more favors of you, but do you think you could hold off any attack from Nergal for just a bit? I have something I need to do."

Maggie grins with a sparkle in her eyes. "I think ya mean you have someone to do. We've got this lass, go get on with yourselves."

Will gives me a wink. "We've got quite a vested interest in you reclaiming your throne, my lady. What do you think we've been doing waiting around her for all these years?"

He shoos us away toward their little cabin before I even have time to ask what that means. I've always known there was something special about the two of them and I'm going to find out what it is. Later.

I take Joachim's hand and then look each of my other guards in the eye, one by one. "I know all is not forgiven, but I'm asking you to set that aside and both witness my mating, and then join with me as I ascend to my rightful place among the gods."

August grins and leans in to give me a quick but hot and tongue tangling kiss. Whew. Not that I needed any help getting all hot and bothered, but that got my engine revving. He gives Joachim a partially playful slap to the cheek and goes to hold the door to the cabin open for us.

Vas gives me a nip on the lips instead of a kiss and then scrapes his teeth across his mark on my throat. I love the tingles that sends through my whole body, that pools right between my legs. The little pinch he gives my butt as he walks past helps too. He only gives Joachim a nod, but it's his approval nonetheless.

It takes Grigori a little bit longer to decide he's down. I don't get a kiss from him, but he pushes his hand into my hair and grips it tight, forcing me to look up at him. The alpha wolf is in his eyes and it's both protective and wants his dominance too. "If he doesn't make you come a thousand times to make up for denying you the pleasure you've deserved from him, I'll cut off his dick and use it myself."

I smile up at him through my lashes. "I know you will."

"Good. As long as we're straight on that." He releases his grip on me, slides his hand down across my throat and holds his palm over his mark. My skin burns for him and he hisses, the alpha's base instinct in him turning from protectiveness to desire.

Oh, this is going to be fun.

Joachim squeezes my hand. "No pressure then."

I can feel his own nerves that match mine, radiating around us. It's silly because this feels more like our first time together, even though we've claimed each other and mated hundreds of times before. I stand up on my tippy toes and press my body against his. I'd forgotten how delicious it is to have his hard muscles against my soft curves.

I brush my lips across his in a teasing not-quite-kiss. "You have nothing to worry about. The moment you touch me with no reservations, I'll come apart. I've wanted you for far too long, and I don't think I have to tell you how many dirty fantasies I've had about your cock and every bit of my body."

Joachim swallows hard and makes a choking sound. But I also feel exactly how hard he's getting beneath his robes. I can't wait to strip them off and know that this time, he isn't going to hide himself or his desires from me.

"Take me, Joachim. Claim me, mate me, make me yours."

JOACHIM

Fuck. What if I've forgotten how to pleasure her? It's been too many lifetimes since we mated and while my cock has never been harder, I'm not sure what to do with it. I can fuck her, sure. But that's for my pleasure and not hers.

I have lifetimes of orgasms to make up for.

What I do know is that part of the wolf mating ritual has always been about a certain amount of dominance and submission. I asked her once long ago before I'd taken my vows of celibacy for the first time, why she wanted that, and her answer was simple.

In the rest of her daily life, she had to be strong and take responsibility for everyone and everything. She was the strongest, most powerful woman, always finding her way into a leadership role in our world in every single life. In this one aspect, when she was with her men that she knew she could trust above all else, that was the one place she could let go of it all.

She didn't have to be the strong one, she could give up her control. And that turned her the fuck on.

I hadn't felt worthy of her trust back then, and the very next life was the first where I chose not to mate with her. I thought Grigori was going to kill me for that decision. He almost did.

Now for the first time in far too long, I could give her what she wanted once again. Starting immediately.

"As you wish, *boginya*." I wrap my hands around her waist and do the one thing that I know gets her going every time. I pick her up like the princess that she is. I love the weight of her in my arms and if she'd let me, I'd carry her around the rest of my life.

She giggles and puts her hands around the back of my neck to pull me down for a proper kiss. At first she keeps her lips closed, and I know what she wants.

"Don't think you can be disobedient now. I'll have you on your knees praying for a kiss and your orgasms if you even try." I bite her bottom lip and push my way into her mouth with my tongue. She moans so sweetly that I could fucking come right then and there.

I want nothing more than to take her on the altar we've made for her in the blooming trees in the woods. That is what would make this moment perfect. If we could claim each other in the ways of worshiping her in ancient times, I could want for nothing more. But the sooner I get her to a bed the better, not only because of the imminent threat of Nergal, but for my own selfish need to be inside of her at last.

When we finally step outside of the barn, the island has changed so much I don't even recognize it. Gone is the ice and snow, and a warm summer evening has bloomed in its place. The constant cover of clouds is gone and the stars twinkle more brightly than I've seen in any of my lifetimes.

The only thing missing is the glow of the full moon.

That's only because I'm holding the moon herself in my arms.

I hurry the twenty steps to the cabin where the others are waiting. Vas ushers us inside, and both Taryn and I gasp at the sight before us. I don't know when and I don't know how, but the interior of the cabin has been transformed. It is no longer a well-lived-in room that functions as living, dining, and kitchen, but now so closely resembles the temple of Ningal at Uruk, I forget how to walk, talk, or even breathe.

The walls are draped in vines of moon flowers that glow with her blue light, that is all directed at a table, nay an altar, in the center of the room. Nothing more, nothing less. Simply a place to worship. To worship her.

Grigori is the first to step up to the altar and drops his robes. August and Vasily follow suit.

I step up to the altar, set Taryn on her feet beside me, and look to my alpha, waiting for his cue.

For the first time since I admitted my wrong doings,

the anger is gone from his eyes. "Ready, Guard of the House of the Divided Moon?"

"I am." As like never before.

He nods to Taryn and begins the ritual. "We gather together in this, our sacred circle to honor the Goddess of the Moon who bestowed upon us the very nature of our wolves and gave us the light by which to find our way to our true fated mates."

He is using the old ceremonial words, if not the old language, that I have spoken three times before. Once for each of them. "If your fated mate be here, declare your claim on them and let your pack know that they are yours and that you belong to them."

Magic as old as time sparkles through me. Taryn presses her hand over my heart just as she did with August, Vasily, and Grigori. She speaks first and I'm grateful because I'm too overwhelmed to say a thing. "I claim you, Guard of the House of the Divided Moon, as my mate. You are mine and I am yours for all time."

Grigori takes my hand and places it over Taryn's heart, but he does not pull away. August puts his hand on top, and then Vas completes the union. I repeat back the words, claiming her for myself, for all of us. "I claim you, Goddess of the Moon, as my mate. You are mine, you belong to us all, and I am yours, as are they, for all time."

My wolf delights at finally getting to claim her and I'm so close to shifting, feeling so free. I throw my head back and howl my pride, my happiness, and my desire for her into the far reaches of the night. August joins his howl and then Vasily's voice joins us and echoes through the night. Grigori lifts his face to the sky and he too blesses this union with his bay to the moonless night.

The howls resound through the unexpected sanctuary and even though we aren't in our new sacred circle of the moon, I feel her blessings. But they grow even more when each and every wolf on the island lifts their voices up and sings the song she gave to us to worship her and the gifts she's bestowed upon our people.

I realize then that we are in a sacred circle. The whole of this island that's always been damned is our sacred circle and a little more of Rasputin's curse, and Nergal's pursuit of innocence is broken.

I'm the first to stop howling because there's something very important I need to do. I drop my mouth to Taryn's throat and whisper against her lush skin. "I love you, my queen, my goddess, my Taryn."

I scrape my teeth across the spot that's been calling to me for an eternity, and relish the deep, sensual moan that comes out of her mouth. "You want me to mark you, right here, right now, don't you?"

"Yes, Joachim. Please."

"Even though you asked so nicely, you'll just have to wait. Because when I mark you, my cock is going to be buried deep in your wet cunt, because I want to feel the first orgasm I give you."

She wobbles in my arms and I hold her tight to keep her upright. "Then don't make me wait any longer. Claim me, take me."

I would love nothing more than to drag this out, fulfilling every one of her desires, but I won't with Nergal's presence weighing over us. Once she'd defeated him, and I know she will, then I'll fulfill every dirty desire she has. With a gentle, but direct shove, I push her back into Grigori's waiting arms.

He can't help it, and wraps his hand around her throat, lifting her chin. Her focus is on him, and it's the opportunity I need. I shift just a few claws and use them to rip open the robes she's wearing, exposing her plump breasts to me. She gasps, but I don't give her even a second before I yank the shreds off her body, revealing every pillowy curve of her body to us. "On your knees, *boginya*."

Grigori gives me a quick side-eye, but I know what I'm doing. I know what she wants from me.

She drops to her knees, the robes padding the hard table beneath her. I push my hand into her hair and tilt her head back so she's looking up at me. I'm the only one still dressed and we both feel the power in this exchange. "Open my robes, Taryn. Take out my cock and see just how ready I am for you."

She licks her lips and reaches her hands into the folds of fabric. As she splits them open, August and Vas each grab a shoulder and drop the coverings to my elbows, making way for her to touch me.

Taryn wraps her hand around the base of my cock and leans forward, her lips parted, and I think I'm about to die. I've dreamed of fucking her mouth. I want to come down her throat, I want to come on her body. I want the evidence of my claim everywhere.

But even more, I want to come inside of her as I mark her, claim her, take her body and give her mine. I wrap her fist with my own and hold her mouth mere centimeters from the tip of my cock. She whimpers and I almost give in.

We both need just a little something to satisfy this craving that we won't get to fulfill today. Slowly, I pump our two hands up and down my shaft watching her eyes follow the movements. It only takes a few strokes before the first drops of precum pool at my slit. "Lick it up, Taryn. But nothing more. I want to feel your tongue on me, see you taste what is yours, but don't take more than I'm allowing you to have."

"Yes, Father."

Oh, holy fuck. Why did she have to go and call me that? I still both of our hands and grit my teeth as I watch her little pink tongue dart out and lap at the bead growing on my cock. The wolf inside of me snarls and growls inside, pushing me to thrust forward and shove my cock into her mouth and all the way to the back of her throat.

I let one of those snarls out as she pulls my seed into her mouth and sucks her own bottom lip in with it. "You want more, don't you, my little lamb?"

She nods and her tongue pokes out again, just as I thought she'd do. "Ah, ah, ah, naughty girl. I didn't give you permission for more than that taste, so now you'll have to face my punishment."

Her eyes go dark with desire, and how I want to play these games with her for hours, taking her to the edge of her desires, and keeping her there until we're both praying for relief. This is all we'll get for this first time. I silently promise her so much more. "August, Vasily, hold her down for me, and Grigori, give her a good spanking to warm her ass up for me."

I turn my back, dying to see the looks on all their faces, but playing my role by turning my back and finally dropping my robes as if readying myself to fuck her. But this is so much more than a ritual fucking. I'm openly giving her my heart, my body, and finally, my soul.

I listen only as I hear Grigori's hand land on her backside and the little whimpers and moans she lets out with each one. If I were a better man, I'd let each of them fuck her now, but I'm not. This time, she is mine. I've watched, I've needed, and I've let each of them have their own marking and claiming of her. It's my turn.

I wait for one more slap and then turn back around to see her deliciously reddened ass up in the air for me and her face pressed to the hard table below. Perfect.

"That's a good girl. Now you'll get what you want." I get down on my knees behind her and grab onto her heavenly hips. Good goddess, she was so soft and lush everywhere from her big, round ass just waiting for me to fuck, to her thick thighs I wanted to bury my cock between. The dimples in her flesh, the stretch marks where her skin couldn't contain her exquisite curves were all like the best aphrodisiac.

How had I ever denied myself, or her?

I push her knees open further with my own and press my hand to her back so that she has to arch her back, opening her pussy to me. My senses are overwhelmed with her scent and my wolf is drooling for wanting a taste.

I almost gave in, until she begged. "Please, Father. I need to feel you inside of me."

That was the end of my control. I thrust my cock into her wet cunt until I was buried, and then I fucked her in long, hard strokes, setting up a rhythm.. "Ask, and it shall be given to you. Seek, and ye shall find. Knock, and it shall be opened unto you."

With only a few thrusts, my wolf is satisfied with her submission and is ready to mark her with my seed. But first I would give her the mark for all the world to see that she belonged to me. I push the others aside and pull her upright. My cock is buried so deep inside of her that we both groan as this new angle tightens her inner walls around me.

"Are you going to be a good girl and come for me, *boginya?*" I reach around and slide two fingers between her slippery wet pussy lips and tease her swollen clit.

She bucks against my hand and she's panting with need. "Yes, Father. Yes. I want to come for you."

I'm going to fuck the hell out of that dirty mouth of hers someday. "That's my girl."

The long, hard thrusts from before are gone, and I now I'm fucking her fast and deep. My wolf's knot is rising up and it's bigger than it's ever been before. I'm pushing hard to get it inside of her and we're both on the edge, but I won't let either of us spill over into that blissful climax until her cunt has taken the whole of my knot. We'll be locked together, vulnerable, and bound in spirit and body.

"Come on, good girl, you can take it, come on, let me in, that's it." I thrust hard and her body finally opens for me. I grunt out my words, too overcome to even find my real voice. "Good girl. Fuck, Goddess, you feel so fucking good."

Her pussy quivers around me, her clit pulses between my fingers and with the last bit of control that I have, I press my mouth to her throat and sink my fangs into her delicious flesh.

Taryn explodes into her orgasm, taking me with, and I spill my seed deep into her cunt, into her womb, and cry out my final prayer claiming her as my mate, my one true love.

TARYN

With my mating with Joachim, I am finally free. I see the past, I see the present, I see the future. Our orgasm spread to my other guards who've been stroking their cocks while being witnesses to my final mating. They all spill their seeds and their knots of the wolf swell at the base. While only Joachim's is buried in my body now, satisfying the beast I gifted him with, I will take the others into me soon too.

I chose these four men so long ago to protect me when I was weak and vulnerable, and in return I offered them my devotion, my body, and my love.

They protected me, but they gave me so much more than that. They gave me purpose and a family.

For the first time since I died in Joachim's arms five thousand years ago, my full power floods into me, and the final tears in my memory heal. I know exactly who and what I am, and no one will ever take that away from me again.

Not even the God of Chaos.

He's been waiting until I was in this most vulnerable moment to attack, but that was his greatest mistake. He wanted the essence of what makes me a woman, the purity of the feminine that lives inside of me. What he's never understood is that is exactly what makes me strong.

He's nursing his wounds from my wrath when he killed Joachim, hiding in the shadows. It won't be long before he's ready to attack again, and I want only to lay here a bit longer and snuggle with my mates. But I have real responsibilities to my people now. I will protect them. I will save them. I will sacrifice everything to defeat Nergal if I have to.

In a minute.

There's a knock at the door and someone calls out to us, interrupting my thoughts on how to get rid of Nergal for good. But I'm glad because I also want to focus on freeing my people from the Island of the Damned.

"Ah, ahem. Sorry to intrude, but there's some people here wanting to see ya, and that pesky owl to take care of." The lilt in Maggie's voice, even trying very hard to be discreet, is unmistakable. I always thought her accent was Scottish, as is her mate's, but I recognize it now for what it is.

She's a queen in her own right, and she's exactly the right person to help me end the curse on this island. No cage can imprison her, not even this one. It's a wonder she hasn't busted out already.

I snuggle into Joachim's embrace for just one more moment, and reach out to touch each of my mates. I wouldn't leave them behind, nor would Maggie leave hers. My heart gives a small ping of pain knowing the beautiful sacrifices that our lovers are willing to give for us.

With a deep breath to resolve myself to crawling out of this bubble of love and getting back to work, I magic us all up some clothes. It's easy peasy magic and moon-light squeezy to use my powers now. It wasn't the holes in my memory that needed to be filled, but the ones in my heart.

"Ready to face our new world, my loves?" Once I get everyone out of this prison and take care of Nergal, everyone has a big culture shock coming their way. Not a single one of them has a clue how much the outside world has changed. I mean, the internet alone is going to make their brains explode. I just hope I'm there to see it.

They each give me an affirmative, and I pop us outside where not only are Maggie and Will waiting for us, but so are hundreds of my people. Maggie dips her head in reverence and I give her the same respect. I can't believe I didn't figure out who or what she was before. Her unique beauty and abilities are so obvious now.

Will takes a knee, and I think I liked it better when he didn't know exactly who I was. Inanna always was an excellent matchmaker, and I'm happy to see she's rewarded him with a love match of his own. It does make me wonder if she placed him in my path on purpose. It's not like her to give up someone as powerful as her lion, unless she had a very specific reason for doing so.

If she did, I'm appreciative. He's been the perfect protector of my people while they were trapped here, and I will have to find a way to reward his service.

The rest of the people gathered follow suit. I allow them the moment of veneration, but this isn't ancient times, and I don't want to be worshiped. Except in the bedroom by my mates.

"Thank you, but please rise. I may have changed a bit, but I am still your friend, and don't expect anything more from you than that."

There are rumbles through the crowd, but eventually most of them get up and don't seem to know what to do with themselves. The wolftresses I've come to think of as my girl gang approach us first.

Brave and bold Alida is the first to say something to me. "My lady, it's an honor to be in your presence."

This is the first time in the last five thousand years that anyone besides my mates knows who I truly am. So, I don't have any precedent for how to tell them I don't want to be treated any differently. "You don't have to call me that. I'm still Taryn, I just have a little more power and magic at my disposal now."

"Uh, you're a bit more than that." She snort-scoffs, then covers her mouth and looks as though she's committed a grievous crime. "You gave of yourself so we could be who we are, and I'm... how did you say it... right, I'm kinda freaked out by that."

"Yeah," Bridget continues. She bows her head and holds a low curtsy. "You're a goddess. Our Goddess."

I'm overwhelmed by their adoration and look to my mates for help. August steps in. "She is, but you've always known there was something special about her, haven't you?"

The girls all nod, and look a bit wide-eyed at me.

He pats Alida on the arm. "And yet you befriended her just as you would any other wolftress. Just because she's our goddess, doesn't mean she doesn't still want your friendship."

"Really?" Alida says what's written across all their faces, but while there is surprise written there, I can also see and sense a release of their initial fear.

"Really, really." I'm going to need them to continue to be the girl gang if we're going to defeat Nergal. I may be very powerful now but so is he, especially unhindered by the yolk of Rasputin. We will be evenly matched. The mates, my friends, and this community is what I hope will give me the advantage.

Am I being the goddess they deserve if I put them in danger again? I'm not sure I can do that and respect myself. But do I have a choice?

I take one of Alida's hands in mine, and encourage the others standing near us to join in too, until we're forming a circle. "We've got some more fighting ahead, both to defeat Nergal, but also to get off this island and start new lives. I'm counting on you to be the wolftresses who keep our community safe and glued together the best we can in the coming days, and hopefully, years."

With my words, I imbue each of these already powerful women with just a little more magic. I want them to have everything they've been denied in this imprisoned life. Maggie joins us and I insert her into the circle as well. She's not one of my people, so I can't give her my magic, but she doesn't really need it. It's just nice to have even more girl power on our team.

The wolftresses relax as they accept the magic and their beautiful beasts rise to the surface, howling in a chorus for only our ears. Every bit of power and magic I've given to them and all of my people returns to me, three-fold. My mates join in and soon everyone is raising their voices to the sky.

I can feel the pride and courage in them all, and that gives me the strength to finally destroy the barriers of this prison. The portals set up to keep us contained here pop, one by one, and as the light of the real world shines through, I feel Nergal slink deeper into hiding.

He's utilizing the permanent portal in the old burned down church and I'm almost ready to bring the fight to him. Just as soon as I'm sure everyone I love is free. Now I know exactly where the final battle will take place.

As the final gray veil of the Volkovs' curse burns away, the lushness of the island's true form emerges. It's green and sunny, with rolling mounds, and not of this Earth. We are not in Kansas anymore, Toto.

Maggie lets out a huge sigh of relief and her true form shimmers like an iridescent rainbow come to life. Her lion steps up beside her, his huge beast form unleashed as well, and protects her with his mere presence. The voices of all those around me slowly fade as the spell breaks and I have to giggle as they gawk at our hosts.

I guess if I had never seen a unicorn before either, I would also have my jaw hanging open.

"Maggie, if I knew we would emerge in Sìthean, when the veil dropped, I would have done this another way. I didn't mean to expose you." The Sidhe were very protective of a Queen like Maggie. They didn't like it when too many knew her true form. Too many unicorns were hunted for their magical blood that could heal any wound or curse.

"Auch, it's fine, lass. The people of the derevnya *are my family just as much as the Sithe."* Maggie's voice in my head is like a tinkling of bells.

"Sorry, but I don't entirely understand," August says.

"The Volkovs stole a chunk of Tir Na Nog, one of the seven fae realms, because of this perfect fairy circle smack dab in the middle of this Siberian lake. My people had used the island as a retreat for years." Maggie indicates the circle of houses of the *derevnya*. What were once cozy cabins in a circle, are now clumps of brightly colored mushrooms. The other buildings have become fairy mounds of green grass, and yet it's all still recognizable as the village where everyone lived for so long.

"Will and I were visiting this sanctuary when Rasputin

discovered the magic here, took it, and turned it into the monstrosity of a prison for himself. We've been trapped in this damned place ever since. Then you lot started showing up, and we figured we'd best try to take care of ya if we could."

Joachim tilts his head and I see the gears working. "But legends say unicorns can't be trapped."

Will lowers his chin onto Maggie's mane. *"Legends also say there hasn't been a dragon in the isles since St. George, yet there is one here now, isn't there?"*

We all turn to look at the black dragon we've befriended and brought along with us. He's looking a bit bewildered at his current surroundings. There's no shadow in Sidhe, and I'm sure that's making him pretty damn uncomfortable, but it confirms what I thought.

This is the perfect place to battle Nergal. And that is the exact reason I must not. His chaos and evil would taint this precious land and perhaps even spill over into the other six realms. I won't have it.

I'll have to open a new portal and get back to the part of our island prison that isn't in Sidhe. I already have a connection with Grigori's lair in the remnants of the church. It will be easy to get back there and root Nergal out.

Fae folk poke their heads out from the hills, the flora, and approach us. They greet my people and offer food and drink. One woman comes over and bows to Maggie. "My lady, we are gratified to have you and your mate return to us. We'd all but lost hope of ever seeing the great aon-adharcach again. It is dark times here in Tir Na

Nog. I am so sorry to report, your daughter has gone missing."

Maggie and Will exchange looks as if this isn't actually news to them. She addresses the woman who is clearly a leader in this realm and who feels horrible about having to deliver this sad news. *"Absolve yourself of any guilt, Cait. Her destiny has called her, and in that we cannot interfere."*

Weirdly, she looks over at me and then to the black dragon and while I might be a goddess, I can't read the mind of a unicorn. I don't have a clue what's going on, but I'm pretty sure Maggie and I are going to have some tea together later.

Cait bows her head again to Maggie and looks relieved. "How can we serve you now, my lady?"

"I'm afraid more darkness is coming. Gather those who are willing to fight at our sides and evacuate those that cannot."

"No, Maggie, your people do not have to fight this battle, it is mine alone." She and Will have given enough of themselves.

My mates are instantly around me. Grigori growls in warning and Joachim shakes his head. "Never alone, *boginya*."

Alida steps up and repeats Grigori's sentiment. "Never alone."

Maggie whinnies, and says the same. *"Never alone."*

Well, crapballs. My heart and soul fills with the warmth of family and friendship that even as a Goddess worshiped by thousands, I'd never truly known until now.

I'd finally resolved to go back to the portal to Hell and fight Nergal on my own and now that plan was shot to shit. All because people loved me and I loved them.

Goddess dammit.

Not sorry, Father.

TARYN

With all this ooey, gooey, mushy, gushy, lovely feelings brought on by the love of friends and family, I got a whole new idea. Long ago, I had a family too and I'm about to call on them.

Nergal wasn't going to get the final battle he wanted. I'd promised to tell on him to Ereshkigal, and that's exactly what I was going to do.

But I had a sneaking suspicion that her sister was involved in these shenanigans too. They were constantly bickering even back in ancient times. That's what I got for having daughters.

Yep. Along with the ascension back to my full goddess magic and powers, I also got the motherload of my memories.

Honestly, I hadn't wanted anything to do with either of them even back then. Selfish of me to leave them to their own devices? Yes. But it wasn't like they were some helpless humans. They were goddesses in their own rights. It was my fault, however, for not teaching them how to wield their responsibilities better.

Perhaps we all had to go through the trials of life to learn our lessons. Mine just happened to be a couple thousand lives. It's not like either of them ever reached out to me during those years when I'd been trying to figure out who I was, so I didn't feel too badly about being an absentee mother.

Besides, it was my own daughter's consort who'd been hunting me all along. She was going to be responsible for setting him straight. Not me.

"I know what to do, but it means bringing three fairly dangerous gods into our midst. I can't guarantee nothing will go wrong, so, I guess, everyone just be prepared to stand your ground. Or better yet, hide behind me."

August, Vas, Grigori, and Joachim surround me, one at each of the four points, and take up a warrior's stance. A day ago, even an hour ago, I might have been surprised that they put themselves between me and the potential danger.

I could use my magic to protect some of the wolves and fae who insisted on being here with us, but not while summoning my family. This little trick was going to use all my power. And since that was the case, I wanted a quick top up.

I turned to Joachim, standing behind me in the position of the divided moon. I pulled him down to me and brushed my lips softly across his. He responded with a needy groan and deepened the kiss until we were both breathless. The mark on my neck lit with the reflection of his love. "You have my heart, now and always."

I slipped from his arms and put myself directly in front of Grigori, my Dark Prince of Wolves. He wrapped me up in his embrace and slashed his mouth across mine. He nibbled and bit at my lips, until I wobbled in his grip. His unique dark glow of the new moon pulsed through his mark on my skin and I was the one moaning with pleasure.

"Come here, Princessa." Grigori carefully passed me to Vasily. I pressed my body to his and we stared into each other's eyes until we were both lost in a sensual haze. He tucked my hair behind an ear and kissed his way from the nape of my neck, where his mark of the quarter moon already burned from within, to my mouth. Our tongues danced and tarried, filling me with passion, joy, and promises of so much more to come.

Vas sent me in a perfect spin, right over to August. My sweet, lovely protector, my rising moon. It all started with him, and I wouldn't have it any other way. He smiles down at me and I fall in love all over again. The kiss he gives me starts soft and turns deep and sensual so easily that I don't want to come up for air. As the final mark on my skin, from being claimed by all my mates ignites, that last bit of magic snaps into place and August lets me go, knowing I'm ready.

I stand in the middle of the four of them, and let the magic flow out of me like the beams of the moon. My moonflowers sprout up in a rapid line all up and down the wolves and fae, family and friends, at my back, and their fragrance fills the air. The sunny day turns to night and I am the only light.

"Nergal, God of Chaos, I summon you to me." I put a good amount of fuck-around-and-find-out into my call, because I'm feeling a little spicy and am looking forward to this confrontation.

A portal between Sidhe and Siberia opens and Nergal screeches like a petulant child. Yeah, that's right you ass of a jackass, come and get me.

He flaps his wings, lifting up into the air and swoops around in his chaotic pattern to begin his attack. "Not this time, birds for brains. It's time for you to go straight back to Hell."

I let more of the magic flow through me and bring the Goddess of the Underworld, my daughter, Ereshkigal. In that same thought, I summon her sister Inanna, the Goddess of Love and War to witness and answer for her part in all of this too.

With one last push of power, Ereshkigal walks through the portal, bringing a swath of shadow with her. August, Vas, Grigori, and Joachim tighten the circle around me, not trusting my daughter. Which is fair. She is the Goddess of Death after all. "It's okay, guys. I got this."

Nergal swoops down, and much too late notices his Queen by my side. She frowns up at him and snaps her fingers. With only that small motion he shifts into a human form, and falls to his knee, his head bowed at her side.

"What are you doing here, husband? Why do you attack my mother?"

Nergal says nothing, but hisses. Ereshkigal looks to me for his answer. "Your dickface of a husband has been making my lives quite hellish. Would you be so kind as to lock his ass up in Hell, please and thank you."

Ereshkigal shoots a death glare at Nergal and he shrinks under her wrath. I'm having a bit of a proud mama moment until she turns that cranky face on me. "I'm a bit busy at the moment, mother. Why don't you take care of him yourself if you've finally gotten your powers back. It's about damn time."

Sigh. What is she thirteen? I can't help but roll my eyes at her. "Because he is your responsibility, child. You can choose to take care of this as I've asked, or you can reap my consequences. I brought you into this world, I can take you out."

That's the most mom thing I've ever said. But it is true. I don't know who'd take over the running of the underworld, but I'm sure I could find someone.

Ereshkigal pouts and folds her arms. She's looking much more the crone than I've ever seen her and for a minute, I almost feel sorry for her. Which is my mistake.

"I'll do as you ask, but I want something in return."

Oh, here we go. "Tell me what you want, and we'll see."

"Stay out of my business with Inanna."

In a poof of rainbows, Inanna appears before us all

with a very colorful dragon at her side. I look around to see where our friend the black dragon has gotten to so I can ask if he knows this one and if he's trustworthy. But Jett is nowhere to be found.

He must have skedaddled when Ereshkigal showed up. I should have warned him. He wouldn't want to get coerced back to Hell. Hopefully, he finds what he needs out in the wide world. Perhaps he'll run into Maggie's daughter and return her to Sidhe.

"Inanna, you're late. Who is this?" My wolves growl at the dragon. They don't seem to like him much.

"Mother, nice to see you with your powers back. This is my mate Kur, the First Dragon." The dragon beside her winks at me and waggles his eyebrows. I am both charmed and irritated at the same time. Which is of course exactly the kind of mate Inanna would choose for herself.

"Mother, she murdered my first husband." Ereshkigal doesn't even wait for or say, *hello, how are you*, before she starts bickering with her younger sister.

Sigh.

Inanna isn't any better. "I did not touch Gugalanna. Enkidu and Gilgamesh slayed him."

Shadow bubbles up around Ereshkigal's feet as it often does when she is upset. "Because you sent them to kill your little pet when he brushed you off."

"Well, I said I was sorry, sentenced Enkidu to death to prove it, and I came to the funeral." Inanna's elements go a bit haywire and snowflakes blow around our heads like wasps. "You hung me from a meat hook and stole my first born son."

Her mate wraps his tail around her and her elements calm. Hmm. Interesting. Maybe he is a better mate than I took him for. They have at least one child together and I take a moment to open my mind to this mate of hers. Ah, they have many children together, and they are grieving the loss of one of them. Among the feelings he lets me access is a great deal of love for my Inanna. Not unlike that which my mates and I feel for each other.

That I can work with.

Nergal on the other hand remained on his knees and didn't do a thing to support Ereshkigal. Not that she needed him to defend her, but we all wanted to know our mate had our back. She continues on her defensive as if he isn't even there.

Ereshkigal has her nails out now and points them at Inanna. "As a replacement for you in Hell when you snuck out. Nobody leaves the Underworld little sister. He's mine now."

I snap my fingers and dampen both of their powers temporarily as a reminder that I am still here and I am the mother. "Daughters, enough. First of all, get with the times and get more modern names. No one even speaks Sumerian anymore. Grow up."

Geez, they're such old fuddy-duddies. I may be their mother, but I feel about five thousand years younger in spirit than they are. Both of my daughters could use a stint on Earth living as a human. I just may have to arrange that.

"Secondly, you've brought more than enough suffering on those that would worship us and I will not stand for more of your bickering. Don't make me send you to your rooms." Granted that wouldn't exactly hurt them since Ereshkigal's realm was the entire underworld and Inanna's was the heavens. Ugh. How did I end up with two such selfish children?

I'm blaming their father. Which is a story for another time. I wound up with my guards for a reason.

Inanna was, and is, impetuous and a bit greedy, but I like this mate she's found for herself. He's changed her, even if she's reverted to her selfishness in this moment. He will be good for her while she learns the lesson of what it means to sacrifice for the good of her children.

I will watch that with interest.

But my poor Ereshkigal hasn't yet learned what real love is. She's hardened her heart. I suppose having one bull-headed husband and then utter chaos as a second consort hasn't helped. If Inanna wasn't so stroppy I'd have her help me find the right mate for her sister.

The two looked at each other and then at me. In unison they apologize. "Sorry, Mother."

"Good. You two need to learn to solve these problems on your own. I'm not getting involved." Inanna opened her mouth to protest, but I shut it up with one look. "Nor are my people. Don't you dare involve the wolves in your little feud anymore. Do you see what kind of grief it's caused me? Five thousand years is enough to make me want to end both of you. Do you hear me?"

"Yes, Mother."

Hmm... somehow I didn't believe it.

"Good. Now Ereshkigal, I've said I won't get involved, so send your consort back to Hell, and I expect you to keep him there. If I see him on the mortal plane again, or if he even thinks about harassing me or my people, I will call your grandfather."

She rolls her eyes at me and I almost expect her to stick out her tongue. I don't care how irritated she is, as long as she keeps her stupid boy toy under control and far away from me.

"And Inanna." I don't know what I am to do with her.

"Uh-oh, Mother. Gotta run." She cupped her hand to her ear as if she had mortal hearing. "Kur needs to use the little dragon's room. Nice to see you again, bye."

She pops back through her portal, Ereshkigal stomps her foot, glares at me, and then does the same. If the two of them hadn't grown up in five thousand years, they weren't going to now just because I wanted them to. Fine, as long as they left me and my people alone, I didn't care.

Maggie sidles up next to me. "Well, kids are fun, aren't they?"

"If you say so." I certainly wasn't having any more.

"That dragon certainly was a handsome fellow. If I didn't have a sexy lion waiting for me, I'd take a bite out of his scales." She giggles and I can't help but laugh at her. "So what will you do now? You and your people?"

Oh, shit. It's my job to take care of them now. I gently touch their minds and see that most just want to go home if they can.

They can't. So many have been imprisoned here for hundreds of years and their homes as they knew them don't exist anymore. "For those of you who want to start a new life, I know of three very good and righteous alphas who will take anyone who is true of heart into their packs."

I open a portal to my last home in Crescent Bay. Niko Troika is in for a surprise, but I expect the Wolf Tzar to be able to handle any kind of situation for his people. Even one this extraordinary. As soon as I take care of some other business, I'll make my way back to America to help these refugees get settled as best as I can.

Many of the prisoners of the Volkovs look a bit shocked, but I push a little bit of calm and confidence into their minds and most make their way to, and then through, the portal. We'll follow behind soon and I'll need to talk to Niko right away to make sure we find a place for everyone.

I imagine he'll be a bit shell shocked when I show up.

Alida, who I have a lot of affection for, has clearly been made spokes-wolftress for the band of stranglers. "Is it okay if some of us stay here? Without the endless winter, this isn't such a bad place."

"Well, that's not entirely up to me as this is not our realm, is it, Maggie?" I turn back to the Queen of Tir Na Nog and smile.

"Auch." Maggie returns my smile and snuggles up close to her mate. "I'd be happy for any of your people to take refuge in my land."

"We can stay if we want? Even though this isn't our realm?" Alida's eyes danced and I could practically see the possibilities blooming in her mind.

"Of course. We've been family for a long time, lass. I'd be sad if you did leave."

With that settled, I turn to my own mates. "Up for one more adventure with me, my loves?"

I get such dazzling, self-assured, promising smiles from all four of them that my heart skips a beat. This life is going to be our best one yet.

TARYN

Joachim slips his hand into mine and I find a slip of paper folded there. "I just remembered I was supposed to give you this from Inanna. She said you'd know what to do with it."

I look at the missive and then let it disintegrate into the rainbow dragon scales it was actually made of. "Looks like we've got a little trip to Hell to make later. I knew she couldn't leave well enough alone."

August, Vas, and Grigori all make a face at me for that plan and I can't blame them. "Don't worry, I'll just pop down to run this errand and be right back."

Grigori raises an eyebrow at me. "I'll give you five minutes."

It shows just how much he's grown that he truly trusts me to do this all on my own. Although, I have no doubt he'll wear a path in the grass pacing until I get back. Adorable.

"And what will you do if I'm back late?" Two can play his game. It's one I rather enjoy.

Joachim answers for him. "A spanking for every minute you're late."

I'll be sure to be at least five or ten late then.

I open my powers and find who I'm looking for. The girl is feeling small, lost, and alone, and I decide to take her a present. Because I cannot save her from her fate and she's got a hard destiny. She will change the world, and I promise both her and myself to do what I can to make her life a little brighter while she undergoes the trials ahead of her.

I pluck a star down from the sky and put it on a dangling cord. It looks a bit like the Christmas ornaments I hung on the trees in my happier childhoods. But I also slice her a sliver of the moon and fashion her a sharp dagger. A girl should have the tools to defend herself when she needs to.

I did promise I wouldn't interfere, but my girls are bit manipulative, and I can play that game too. With a blink, I'm just outside one of the small caves she's claimed for herself. But not in today's underworld. I've jumped back in time several hundred years to not long after she was captured.

She's already drawn upon the magic of her ancestors, witch and wolf, making her a little bit mine. She may be the daughter of a dragon, but she's got a long line of supernatural power in her blood, witch, and wolf. It's the only reason she'll survive under such harsh conditions.

She sees me through the spell she's cast to keep Ereshkigal out, and studies me for a long time before she drops the shield and lets me in. "Who are you?"

"I'm Ningal."

"Oh, you're grandmother."

I suppose I am. "I've come to bring you some presents."

"Yes, give them to me, they're mine." She sits on a bit of the stone carved out from the wall and holds out her hands.

Her lack of manners doesn't bother me. It's not like her own mother has been allowed to raise her beyond her first few years, and that makes me so sad that I want to simply whisk her away. But if I did, she wouldn't be able to build up the strength she's going to need to save her world.

I hand her the dagger first. "This dagger is very sharp and will never go dull. Can you use it wisely?"

"Of course I can." There's a very distinct *duh* in her voice and I forget for a moment she's much older inside than her few human years.

"Good. This one is to bring some light into your life when you need it." I dangle the star and this time she takes the gift with much more reverence.

The star and the dagger have the magic inside that will allow her to save the world someday. She'll help bring the dragons and the wolves together in their darkest hour.

"I want more. Please." Her face flushes, and I'm not

sure she's ever used that word before. She feels the power of the magic and its draw. She won't understand why she can hear more, see more, and be more than everyone else around her.

"I'll bring you more, but you have to promise never to tell anyone that I was here. I'm cheating a bit by visiting you."

She nods. "I promise."

"I've got one more gift for you." My time away is more than up, and while I don't want to leave her, I know that Grigori and the others will be worried if I don't hurry along.

She holds out her hand again, but I shake my head. "This one isn't a thing, but something else. It's a gift to say thank you for helping my wolves when they need your help someday soon. Okay?"

She narrows her eyes at me and I touch my finger to her forehead. With one brilliant burst of my moon's light, I push one more bit of my magic into her soul.

It won't make any sense to her for a while, but once she is ready to leave Hell, Inanna and Ninshubar will help her use it to find her own mate. It's the least we'll all owe her for the sacrifices she'll have to make.

Her eyes flutter, and she sighs, her body relaxes, and I help her to lay on her makeshift bed.

"Good night, Fallyn, sleep tight. I'll see you again soon, little lady bug." I establish her protective wards so that no one can disturb her rest and then shift back to the current day, pop back up to Sidhe and my mates.

August wraps me in his arms and holds me close. He doesn't say anything, and it's exactly the support that I need from him. When I'm ready, I extract myself and look toward the portal.

"Ready, boys?" We have a new life waiting. One that I can't wait to get started.

"Yes, but for what? I'm not sure what to do with myself now that we're not fighting to protect you," August says, but I could tell by the waggle of his eyebrows he knew exactly what he wanted to do.

Vas joined in. "Yes. I can think of a few things."

Grigori snorted but the dancing wolf in his eyes said he was game for some, umm, games. Joachim rubs his hands together and I think he's already counting those spankings.

The five of us wave to Maggie, Will, and the wolves staying behind in Sidhe. We make two or three real quick stops directed by Grigori to pick up some things he says we'll need for our new life, and then finally step out of my portal to Troika lands. We pop up on the beach, along with the rest of my people. They've huddled together in small groups and while I get the feeling of some nervousness, they too are excited for this new life.

"Come on, everyone. I've got a favor or two to call in." We make our way up the beach to what used to be an old, yellow, dilapidated inn. It's had quite a bit of work done since I last saw it, as have the cabins surrounding it. I hope Heli and Kosta are ready to have a full house.

I signal to the group to wait on the porch and walk up

the restored front steps and into the double doors of the new Bay Inn. I look around at the light and breezy ocean-themed decor of the lobby. It's both homey and vacationy at the same time. There's an old friend working behind the counter, but she's tapping away on the computer and hasn't spotted me yet. "Is there any room at the inn?"

Heli spins around, searching for the voice, finally finds me, and her eyes go from normal surprised to holy shit surprised. "Taryn? Oh my God, is it you? Where have you been?"

"Hi Heli. It's a long, long story." A really, really long story.

"Something has changed about you." She looks over my shoulder and her eyes go even wider. "Uh, I think I can see what."

"Heli, meet August, Vasily, Joachim, and Grigori, my mates."

"Lucky girl." She winks at me. "Nice to meet you all."

Time to get down to business. "It seems I'm homeless, now that Niko and Zara have taken over the Crescent pack."

Heli makes an uh oh face, but I smile so she understands I'm not upset. "Oh, uh, I'm sure Niko would love to talk to you about that."

"Yes, I will want to chat with them, but when you call them," which I'm sure she will immediately if not sooner, "please assure them, I'm not here to challenge him. I'm very content with all that I have. I do have some people who'll need his help."

It's really interesting to see how the wolftress in her is reacting to my presence. Somehow her newly transformed beast knows who I am, but hasn't let the human woman part of her in on the secret yet. My original gift had transformed all my people, and for a while, they kept to our own kind. But it didn't take long for one of my wolves to fall in love with a human.

Humans are so interesting and unique that when my gift is transferred to them, it doesn't always result in the ability to shift. I wonder if there is a common denominator to the ones that do, and the ones that develop other supernatural abilities.

I'd be paying a lot more attention when I meet other new mates of my wolves in the future.

"So, for real though. I really am homeless and was wondering if you had a room, or rooms, available for us."

"Of course." She taps on her computer for a second and says, "I think I have just the thing. We just finished refurbing the old Presidential suite. But I hate that name, so I'm calling it the Goddess suite. How long would you like to stay?"

"Umm, indefinitely. I'll need a home base while I figure out where I belong in the world now." I'd love to be somewhere nearish to the area I grew up in, but I don't think I'd actually be comfortable back in my not-father's old territory. It's better off with Niko and Zara.

"Okay," she tapped the keyboard a few more times. "I'll just charge that to Niko, since you know, he took over your pack, and umm, you know, he's the Wolf Tzar now and all. I think he can afford it."

"Well, I'm going to need more than just that suite." I wave to the guys and they bring in the first wave of other guests I'm hoping she can accommodate. "I've got some friends who don't have anywhere to call home either."

Heli takes a quick peek out the window, then down at her computer. "Uh, yeah. Good thing we haven't opened yet. Anyone up for some beach camping?"

She was so cute and kind. "Thanks, yes. We'll take anything and everything you've got. And if you're up for a bit of trade, I've got some old family heirlooms I could give you to cover the first few days or so."

I pulled out a ring made of emeralds and diamonds that Grigori had given to me when I'd been Katherine the Great. I may have turned an entire room of the Winter Palace into a jewelry box, but he had hidden away even more precious items that he'd intended to bolster my wealth and position in future reincarnations. I'd only had one more life in Russia after that, and I'd only lived to seventeen and in an extremely privileged life. I hadn't needed the fortune he'd amassed.

It was going to come in handy now if I was to live among the humans and my people. I pressed the ring into Heli's hand and she shivered. "Holy shit, Taryn, is this real?"

"Yep. That should cover any expenses we might incur. Although, these guys eat like they haven't been fed in hundreds of years, so let me know if you need anything more." I wasn't going to be wanting for money anytime soon, and now neither were Heli and Kosta.

Heli tapped away on her computer, handed out keys, and called back to her kitchen for Kosta. When he came up to the desk, he looked around at all the people, then at Heli, then at me. I gave a little wave, and he dropped to one knee and bowed his head.

Heli laughed. "It's just Taryn, sweetheart. Well, and a whole bunch of her friends. Oh, and her four mates."

Kosta didn't lift his head, but spoke out the side of his mouth at his mate. "That might be Taryn, *zaika*, but she is also the Goddess of the Moon."

Heli tilted her head one way, then the other, and I give her a little wave. "That's cool as shit. I think we'd better call up Gal, Zara, and Selena and invite them over for some tea. Or, uh, maybe something stronger."

"Yes, let's do that. But maybe tomorrow?" It had been so long since I'd lived as a goddess and not a mortal, that I actually wasn't entirely sure what to do about my old friends and connections. But I could think about that tomorrow. For now, I knew I wanted to spend a lot of time rekindling a lot of old fantasies.

Oh. I had a great idea. I leaned over the counter to whisper to Heli and she snort giggled when I asked about their in-room entertainment.

"Like I think you'll need it." She handed over the keys to the suite and pointed us up the grand staircase. In true guard fashion, August picked me up, threw me over his shoulder and sprinted up the stairs three at a time. He didn't set me down, despite my protests and squeals, until we were at the door to the suite.

"Come on boys. You've been locked up for all of the modern era and I'd like to introduce you to running hot water, a luxurious hotel room, room service hamburgers and fries, and maybe pay-per-view porn."

Joachim lifted me up into his arms again and kissed my brand new mark of his wolf. "I don't know what any of that means, but where you go, we go. So let's go pay to view porn.

And we did. For an entire day.

In the light of the full moon that evening, I snuggled deep into the arms of two of my lovers, fingers intertwined with others. I am powerful, I am a Goddess and I am worshiped.

While others may pray to me and give me thanks for the gifts I've given them, I too am thankful. I close my eyes, and send my gratitude out into the universe. It hasn't been an easy journey, but I wouldn't have it any other way, because it's made me who I am.

I love myself, I love my mates, and I love my fate.

My fate with my wolf guards is my very own happy ever after.

WANT MORE WOLVES? Pop over and read the Alpha Wolves Want Curves series and see Taryn's life before she found her fate.

Start with Dirty Wolf.

Wondering what's going on between Inanna and Ereshkigal? Or how about Maggie and Will's daughter? Just where did Jett the black dragon disappear off to? And what is going to happen to Fallyn?

You're gonna want to read Dragons Love Curves!

Start with Chase Me.

Get it now, or turn the page for an excerpt from chapter one.

EXCERPT FROM CHASE ME

CHAPTER 1: ALWAYS THE WEDDING PLANNER, NEVER THE BRIDE

Agh. Ciara's feet ached, her back was stiff and the headache she'd staved off with some ibuprofen four hours ago was rapidly creeping back behind her left eyeball. Nothing like the sweet pains of victory.

One more commission like this and she could afford to take that beach vacation she'd been promising Wesley for the past three years.

"Oh Sarah, there you are." The bride's mother, who was reason number one, two, three, and forty-three for said headache, waved her over. Mother-of-the-Bridezilla paid the bills, so Ciara pasted on her most helpful smile and greeted the table.

"Hello everyone. Having a nice time?"

Headache mom turned to the couple sitting next to her. "Bill, Thi, this is Sarah, the wedding planner. You simply must book her for your Linh's wedding. She is the best—always available for her clients. I called her last week at two in the morning when I simply knew that Bethany needed to have three more wedding cakes at the reception. Sarah never says no."

Oh, great. That's what she wanted to be known for. Being the slut of the wedding planner world.

"Well, I like to hear that. We want our baby to have everything she wants for her wedding. No expense spared. Do you have a card, Sarah?"

"It's Ciara actually, and yes, of course." She handed Bill, who she could already tell was wrapped around his daughter's little finger, a card. Bill handed the card to his wife. "Let me write your time and date on the back for you."

She pulled a pen out of her kit. Always prepared, true to her Girl Scout roots. She scribbled on the back of the card.

"Ciara Mosley-Willingham. Do you own Willingham Weddings, dear?"

Sigh. Not yet. Not ever if her mother had anything to do with it. "That honor goes to my mother, Wilhelmina."

"Ah, I see. Well, nepotism has its benefits." The table all chuckled at Bill's little joke.

Benefits schmenefits. If only they knew.

"I've got an appointment that just opened up for two weeks from Monday. Will that work to bring Linh in for a consultation?"

"Two weeks?"

She nodded. "I'm afraid the next available is in August."

The couple glanced at each other. They were not used to waiting patiently. Most of her clients weren't.

"That's almost three months from now."

Headache mother raised a glass of champagne. "You wanted the best. Better get her while you can."

Thi raised an eyebrow, trying to intimidate Ciara. Not gonna happen. Ciara gave the mother her award-winning account-getting smile.

Thi gave in. "We'll be there."

Bali with Wesley, here she comes. If she could ever get him to ask her out in the first place, and in another three years when her schedule cleared up. Not that her mother would ever allow her to take a vacation, but at least now she had a plan to get that date with the hunk of the office.

Ciara made her rounds, vying for a chance to run into Wes with the good news. News that should be celebrated, with a night on the town, a nice dinner, some satin sheets.

She checked in with the catering staff and found out he was in the kitchen. Wes, in a perfect three-piece suit with the purple pocket square and matching vest, just about took her breath away. How any man this good looking would be interested in her blew her mind.

By interested, she meant he flirted with her constantly at the office but hadn't ever asked her out. Ciara had made it perfectly clear she was willing and available.

He hinted, she smiled and nodded, and then nothing.

A girl could only wait so long for the man of her day dreams to make a move.

"Hey babe." He kissed her on the cheeks while holding his cell phone to his ear. "We've got a champagne shortage crisis on our hands."

No need to stress. Cool, calm, and collected. Always. "No problem. I'll bring in the secret back-up case I keep in my car."

Wes hung up his phone and winked at the disheveled waiter with the empty tray. "Told you Ciara would swing some of her magic."

He was such a sweet talker. She hoped he was a dirty talker too. Whoa, wait. Down girl. She had to get a date with him first. "I'll go grab it, but the bouquet toss is in a few minutes. Go chat up all the single girls and talk them into standing up to catch the bouquet."

One wink or an eyebrow waggle from him and they'd all be smashing each other in the face to catch those flowers whether they wanted to or not.

"I'll go get the champagne, you go catch the bouquet." Wes shook his head and shivered.

Lots of bouquets were in her future, but not for catching. Always the wedding planner, never the bride. Yet.

Here goes nothing, or something, or gah, just ask him.

"Hey, I just landed the Barton wedding. We should celebrate."

Wes grinned. "You are going to make us all zillionaires. I cannot even keep up."

Okay, this was going well. Ask him. "So, you'll go out with me to celebrate?"

"You bet."

He didn't hesitate even a little. She should have asked him months and months… and months ago.

"Are you free on Wednesday?" They had weddings on the weekends, but she hoped she didn't sound lame for suggesting a weeknight.

"Nope. But, I could do Thursday. Dinner, drinks, and I know the greatest place to go clubbing."

Dinner, drinks, and dancing. Perfect.

She wanted to jump up and down and clap her hands.

Not appropriate.

Be cool.

Ciara drew upon her inner cucumber-ness. "Sounds great."

Enough said. Right? Yeah, that was fine. She didn't want to look overly enthusiastic. She'd save that for the in-bed portion of their evening.

Geez, she needed to get her mind out of the gutter. She'd gone from dinner and dancing to handcuffs and blindfolds in seconds. Oh, please let him be at least a little kinky.

"Ciara?"

"Yeah?" She blinked, still caught up in her fantasy sex life with Wesley.

"You feeling alright? You look a little flushed."

She'd be fine and dandy if she could get the real Wesley into her fantasy life. "Yep. Great. Go grab that champagne and get it on ice."

"You're the best, you know that, right?" Wes grabbed her in a bear hug and danced her around. He jerked back and rubbed at his chest. "Ouch, your necklace bit me."

"Oh, geez. Sorry." Ciara put her hand over the colorful pendant she'd gotten a few days ago. She didn't feel anything sharp.

"Pretty but painful, doll." Wes examined the charm, staring a scant inch above Ciara's boobs. "It would go with everything. Where'd you get it?"

Damn. She'd kind of hoped Wesley had sent it. Not likely, but she was ever hopeful. Must be from her mother, who rarely gave gifts. Weird.

"Oh my god, Ciara, there you are. I'm getting a divorce, or is it an annulment? Whatever. George is such an ass. I want out of this marriage right now." The bride ran into the kitchen and faux collapsed into Ciara's arms.

She glanced at Wes, who shook his head and smirked. He mouthed the words good luck and backed away from them.

This woman wasn't the first newlywed to freak out at the reception and she wouldn't be the last. Ciara had a long track-record of calming them down and helping them focus on what was important, their happily ever afters. Wesley called her the bride whisperer.

Ciara put a hand on the bride's arm and sent all the happy calming positive thoughts she could muster. They took a deep breath together.

"You can do this. Everything is going to be fine."

The bride nodded, looking a little dazed and repeated Ciara's words. "Everything is going to be fine."

A few hours later, the bride and groom had more than made up. The bouquet was tossed, the champagne chilled and toasted, the candles blown out, all topped off by the perfect sunset.

At two in the morning, Wes escorted the last of the drunken groomsmen to the limos they'd arranged to drive the non-sober home and Ciara collapsed into the nearest chair.

If she took her shoes off now, they were never ever going back on, but she'd limp home barefoot rather than take one more second in her not-so-high heels.

A lonely uneaten piece of wedding cake had been calling to her ever since she saw the fit groomsman walk away from it several hours ago. After that marathon wedding and reception, she needed a good sugar fix.

"Stop right there, thief." The deep rumble of a male voice halted the fork midway to her mouth. Sounded like he was back for his dessert. Oh God. How embarrassing.

"I'm just doing a bit of quality control. Have to make sure the cake is up to Willingham Weddings standards."

Please don't let him mention the fact that the wedding

was over. Ciara turned to give the groomsman her best don't mind me I'm just the chubby, dateless, wedding planner stealing a piece of leftover cake smile. The man-slash-movie-star-slash-romance novel cover model standing three feet behind her had his arms crossed and a mad as hell glare on.

He wore a tight black t-shirt, dark jeans and a beautiful bright green crystal on a cord around his neck, so he wasn't the groomsman, or any other guest of the Ketcher-Fast wedding. She'd remember all that fantasy material.

He glanced down at the glowing charm at his throat and stilled. He faltered for a second and had to grab on to a chair to keep his balance.

Great. Another drunk guest and all the limos were gone. No way was she driving him home herself. Hmm. Well, maybe. He was awfully sexy and all those daydreams she'd had about Wes all night suddenly starred this magnetic stranger.

Until he growled at her. "I don't give a damn about the cake, unless that is where you've hidden my goods."

"Your goods?" The only goods Ciara could comprehend at the moment were six, or maybe eight, of the most beautifully defined abdominal muscles in the whole Four Corners.

He crossed the scant yard between them in two strides, hauled her up out of the chair, and got so far into her personal space bubble she could smell his cinnamony breath. A zing whipped through her from every place he touched and strangely, she really wanted to stand up on her tippy toes and press her lips to his, taste that spice, lick up every essence of that erotic flavor.

She might have too if he'd held her for a second longer. But, after searching her eyes, he released her and began pacing, prowling around her, his eyes roving her from head to toe.

He might have the body of a god and she the body of a cupcake, but she would not be intimidated by wandering eyes. "First of all, you have to tell me what brand of toothpaste you use, and second, back up out of my business, buster."

"Do not try to beguile me with your talk of hygiene products, your hair of gold, and your body made for sin. Where have you hidden my Wyr relic, witch?" He stopped circling and stared straight at her butt.

Body made for sin? Was he kidding? Body made of sins, maybe. Namely the sins of Swiss meringue buttercream, chocolate ganache, and too many I Love Lucy reruns. "Stop staring at my tuchis. Whatever you're looking for ain't in there."

She wiggled her backside to emphasize her point. That made her intruder damn irritated, probably that her rear wasn't dropping any evidence of wrong doing based on the growl rumbling from his chest and his eyes glued to her ass.

"Stop enticing me with your curves, thief. You cannot distract me from what is mine."

Ciara cleared her throat, gently at first, but when that

failed to bring his eyes up to hers, she about gave herself a sore throat trying to get his attention.

"Are you ill? I won't have you dying before you tell me where the statue is hidden."

What an asshat. A cute one, but a real douche canoe nonetheless. "I think maybe we've gotten off on the wrong foot here." Ciara extended her hand to him. "I'm Ciara Mosley-Willingham." Her hand hung there for a full count of ten. "And you are?"

He recoiled from her hand. "Wondering what kind of spell you're trying to work on me. Whatever it is, I assure you a Wyvern is immune."

"I was trying to be nice, but I've had a very long and tiring day, so my patience is wearing thin. I don't have your thingy, and I don't know what a why Vern is. I thought for a minute I might help you try to find it, but I'm done now." Ciara turned and began looking for her torturous heels. It would be much more fun to stomp off if there was some clack.

"As am I. If you won't return what you have taken from me I will be forced to bring you before the AllWyr council."

"What the hell?"

He grabbed her hand and pulled her through the ballroom toward a terrace. Good thing she'd already kicked off her shoes or she'd have been tripping all over her feet at the rate he was dragging her away.

"Hey, stop right this instant or I'll bring out the self-defense moves."

"Save your defense for the council. You'll need it."

This dude was seriously a wackadoo. Where was the pepper spray when she needed it? Oh, that's right, still in the bag from the store her mother had insisted they buy in bulk from.

"Let me go."

"Return my relic."

"I'm gonna make you a relic."

"Save your spells, witch."

"Your face is a witch."

The scary man released her and grabbed at his face. When he didn't find anything wrong with it, he narrowed his eyes and glared at her. "Good try, witch. You'll pay for that."

Ciara pivoted and bolted weaving her way between the tables. One second she was zigging and zagging, the next she was airborne.

Great talons gripped her shoulders and a deep whoosh-whoosh-whoosh sounded above her.

She wriggled and screamed, frantically trying to see what was happening above her. Her feet crashed into empty glasses and caught a centerpiece of giant lilies dead-on as she was dragged through the air above the tables.

Before she could even take another breath to scream again, they swooped out of the French doors, over the balcony and into the night sky.

Ciara lost her effing mind as the ground beneath her sunk down into tiny squares of land. She couldn't look any longer, or she'd throw up. So instead she glanced up, not fathoming that she'd see flying above her the giant wings, flapping gracefully through the sky, of a dragon.

JOIN in Ciara's adventures with her Dragon Warrior Jakob in Chase Me

ACKNOWLEDGMENTS

Big thanks to my proofreader, Chrisandra. She probably hates commas as much as I do now. All the remaining errors are all my fault. I'm sure I screwed it up somewhere.

I'm ever grateful to Elli Zafiris and Becca Syme for telling me I'm worth fighting for when I'm sure I've effed up my book and my career. You two are my energy pennies.

I am so very grateful to have readers who will join my on my crazy book adventures where there will ALWAYS be curvy girls getting happy ever afters!

Without all of you, I wouldn't be able to feed my cats (or live the dream of a creative life!)

Thank you so much to all my Patreon Book Dragons!

An enormous thanks to my Official Biggest Fans Ever. You're the best book dragons a curvy girl author could ask for~

Thank you so much for all your undying devotion for

me and the characters I write. You keep me writing (almost) every day.

Hugs and Kisses and Signed Books and Swag for you from me! I am so incredibly grateful for each of you and am awed by your support.

- Helena E.
- Alida H.
- Daphine G.
- Bridget M.
- Stephanie F.
- Danielle T.
- Marea H.
- Marilyn C.
- Mari G.

Shout out to my Official VIP Fans!
Extra Hugs and signed books to you ~

- Jeanette M.
- Kerrie M.
- Michele C.
- Corinne A.
- Deborah S.
- Frania G.
- Jennifer B.

ALSO BY AIDY AWARD

Dragons Love Curves

Chase Me

Tease Me

Unmask Me

Bite Me

Cage Me

Baby Me

Defy Me

Surprise Me

Dirty Dragon

Crave Me

Dragon Love Letters - Curvy Connection Exclusive

Slay Me

The Black Dragon Brotherhood

Tamed

Tangled

Twisted

Fated For Curves

A Touch of Fate

A Tangled Fate

A Twist of Fate

Alpha Wolves Want Curves

Dirty Wolf

Naughty Wolf

Kinky Wolf

Hungry Wolf

Filthy Wolf

The Fate of the Wolf Guard

Unclaimed

Untamed

Undone

Undefeated

Claimed by the Seven Realms

Protected

Stolen

Crowned

By Aidy Award and Piper Fox

Big Wolf on Campus

Cocky Jock Wolf

Bad Boy Wolf

Heart Throb Wolf

Hot Shot Wolf

The Curvy Love Series

Curvy Diversion

Curvy Temptation

Curvy Persuasion

The Curvy Seduction Saga

Rebound

Rebellion

Reignite

Rejoice

Revel

ABOUT THE AUTHOR

Aidy Award is a curvy girl who kind of has a thing for stormtroopers. She's also the author of the popular Curvy Love series and the hot new Dragons Love Curves series.

She writes curvy girl erotic romance, about real love, and dirty fun, with happy ever afters because every woman deserves great sex and even better romance, no matter her size, shape, or what the scale says.

Read the delicious tales of hot heroes and curvy heroines come to life under the covers and between the pages of Aidy's books. Then let her know because she really does want to hear from her readers.

Connect with Aidy on her website. www.AidyAward.com get her Curvy Connection, and join her Facebook Group - Aidy's Amazeballs.

Printed in Great Britain
by Amazon

85233243R00087